LORD OF STONE

D.J. GOODMAN

SEVERED PRESS
HOBART TASMANIA

LORD OF STONE

WWW.SEVEREDPRESS.COM

ISBN: 978-1-925597-63-9

CHAPTER ONE:
THE COURT OF PUBLIC OPINION

"Fuggin' go awuh," Trudy Hollis muttered at the incessant buzzing in her head. For a moment, it did. Then it came back, and after several more bleary seconds, she realized the obnoxious noise wasn't in her head at all. It was her doorbell. It had been so many months since anyone had been around to use it, coupled with the alcohol-induced haze she'd been in for pretty much that whole time, that she'd nearly forgotten what it sounded like.

She raised her head off the carpet, only vaguely aware of the wet puddle of drool her cheek had been in and the rough, scratchy imprint of the carpet on her skin. She wasn't worried about anyone seeing her like this, though, since she had no intention of opening the door.

Trudy slowly pushed herself up into more or less of a sitting position on the floor, checking as she did to make sure that the floor around her crotch wasn't wet again. There would have once been a time when the great and famous Trudy Hollis would have been mortified at the idea of wetting herself. Now she was just relieved that she didn't have to clean the smell out of the carpet yet again.

Again the doorbell. She almost screamed for whoever kept pushing it to just stop already, but caught herself at the last moment. That would do nothing but confirm to the person that she was indeed in her apartment. Maybe if she was quiet, they would eventually think she wasn't here and go away. Sure, she had a little curiosity about who it could be after all this time, but most likely it was just some two-bit journalist that had suddenly remembered she existed and thought she could give a few comments to some three-paragraph follow-up piece on some tabloid website. It would be better to just keep her mouth shut, at least until she could find a bottle that still had some whiskey or something in it and she could

1

return to her haze.

She thought all this as she stood up, or tried to stand up. It was more like pulling herself up using the furniture in order to keep from toppling over again. The hangover was bad this morning (or was it afternoon?), but at least there was no visible sign that she had vomited on anything last night (this morning? Seriously, what the hell time was it?). Her first stumbling steps, though, knocked over a couple of empties that had been next to the couch. There was no way her uninvited guest didn't hear it.

Still, for several seconds Trudy stood absolutely still, hoping the person had somehow missed it.

"Mrs. Hollis-Nelson?" a man's voice called from beyond the door.

"For God's sake," she muttered to herself. Then, loud enough that her intruder could hear her through the door, "No soliciting!"

"Mrs. Hollis-Nelson, I need to speak with you. My employer…"

"Go away or I'll call the cops!" She started toward the door, only getting about halfway before her world started to spin and she had to stop to regain her balance.

"My employer has a proposition for you," the man continued.

"Tell the bastard to learn how to use a phone." And that way, too, it would be easier for her to turn it off and ignore him.

"We tried. Apparently, your service has been turned off?"

Oh. Right. Trudy had forgotten about that. She'd stopped paying her cell phone bill altogether after her fifty-third death threat, the same thing that had caused her to completely abandon the internet. She was still paying her cable bill, but only because all the TV news outlets had moved on to more recent scandals to exploit. To them, Trudy's shame was old news. If she just kept in hiding for another five or six years, maybe she would be able to show her face in public again.

Then again, maybe not.

"That should have been your first clue," Trudy yelled, even though she was standing right at the door now. "Whatever you want, I'm not interested. No comment. No photos. And no more God-damned stalkers. Seriously, go away or I'll call the cops."

There was the audible sound of the man trying to repress a

laugh. "And how do you plan on doing that without a phone?"

Oh for Christ's sake. "Just go away. I've got..." She was going to say she had a gun, but that was the image the media had pasted all over the place of her, wasn't it? Her, a rifle in her hand, and a "cool and uncaring demeanor" on her face, as one national rag had worded it. The last thing she wanted was to use that as a threat and bring that whole mess back to this person's mind.

"Mrs. Hollis-Nelson, if you will just let me come in and speak to you..."

She leaned against the door and sighed. All the fight drained from her voice. "Tell you what. I'll let you in and give you ten minutes, but only if you stop calling me that."

"I'm sorry, stop calling you what?"

"Hollis-Nelson. It's just Hollis now."

There was a long pause from the other side. "I'm so sorry. I should have remembered. Please, Miss Hollis, may I come in?"

It took a surprisingly long time for Trudy to fumble the multiple locks open. She had to still be a little on the tipsy side. That, or she was subconsciously still trying to keep the world out even as she let it in. When she'd finally managed to unlock all four, she let the door swing open a few inches and then walked away, trying to make it look like she didn't actually care who had come calling on her. In truth, despite her blazing hangover keeping her from thinking too clearly, her curiosity was piqued. This man had been more persistent than any attempted visitor she'd had in at least three weeks. He had to be here for something special, at least in his mind.

As she wandered in the direction of her kitchen, hoping to find a beer or something in the fridge that she had previously missed, she casually looked over her shoulder at her visitor. He was African-American like her, but also short and bald. The deep creases in his forehead suggested either a life long-lived or a life short-lived except with lots of frowning. He wore a long, dark coat and tailored suit that brought to mind some kind of government agent, but the suit was of too high a quality for that. Whoever this guy worked for, it was someone who could pay the hired help decent money.

"Drink?" she asked him as she opened the fridge.

He sniffed the air. Although Trudy herself had grown used to it, she was sure the apartment reeked of alcohol and body odor. "Uh, no. Thank you."

That was just as well, since the fridge was empty. As soon as she got rid of this guy, she was going to have to take another trip to the liquor store. Assuming her credit card didn't finally get rejected. She wasn't sure when the last time had been that she'd paid it.

She closed the fridge and turned to lean on the counter, doing her best not to look like she cared that a man was in her apartment wearing a suit that probably cost more than her rent. "So? Go ahead and talk. The sooner you do, the sooner I can tell you to leave."

Instead of saying anything, the man walked further into her apartment and went right for the bookshelf next to her couch. Trudy stiffened. She had the mind often in the last two months to pack away every single thing on that shelf and hide it in the back of a closet. Or maybe even burn them. She'd never gotten around to it, though, as she was often too busy being passed out on the couch.

He reached up to a shelf near the middle, carefully ran a finger across the spines of several books, then stopped with a smile when he seemed to find one that pleased him. He pulled it out and began flipping through it, standing at an angle as he did so that clearly allowed her to see which one it was. *Up Among the Giants*, by Trudy Hollis. One of her earlier works, long before she had temporarily added Nelson to the end of her name.

"I read this one, oh, I think about twenty years ago?" the man said. "The prose was obviously the work of a beginner, but the subject matter was fascinating."

Trudy didn't speak, didn't even look at him. A lot of people had thought the same thing. Although *Up Among the Giants* hadn't been the first book about her work, it had always been the most popular. Or at least it had been before the public turned on her.

He put the book back on the shelf before bending down and looking down at the rest of the books on the shelf. The shelf he'd first been perusing had all been her own books, but the rest of her shelves consisted mostly of reference works, everything from her old college biology textbooks to tour books for the various countries she'd visiting during her travels and studies. He seemed to linger on a Moon Handbook for Uganda before he stood back up and looked her in the eye.

"Quite the life you had," he said. "And quite different from what you're doing now."

"I'm sorry, but who the hell even are you?"

"My name is George Axton."

"Aaaand is that a name I'm supposed to know? Because you came sauntering in here as though you expected me to be impressed or something. And I have to say, it's not happening yet."

"Of course not. I'm just a messenger. Among other things. It's my employer that you've probably heard of. Marvin Irving?"

The name rang all sorts of vague bells in Trudy's head, although it took a while for all the facts to line up in her hung-over brain. "Isn't he... uh, the Bouncer?"

Axton smiled. "He was known as that once. He's better known for other things now, of course."

"Like?"

"Have you ever seen the show *Sell Your Soul*?"

Suddenly, she could put a face to the name, a dark, serious face belonging to a giant of a man in an impeccably tailored suit that would make Axton's look like a garbage bag with holes cut in it for arms. "Oh. He's one of the Buyers, isn't he?"

"That's what he's best known for right now, but I'm sure you know..."

"He's got his hands in everything," Trudy said. "So what, he's sent you here to make some kind of deal with me? Trust me, I don't have any deals for him to get in on the ground floor on."

"I'd be surprised if you did," Axton said. "That's never been your kind of thing. If I remember correctly, you've had opportunities to cash in on your work in the past, haven't you? Wasn't there an offer once to put your name on a line of plushes?"

"Yep. And I told the toy corporation to go fuck themselves. I wasn't going to cheapen what I do just so they could have a famous name on the next version of Beanie Babies."

"And if I still recall correctly, those were your exact words.

'Go fuck yourselves.' And you said it on national television. You ended up losing money thanks to the massive fine the FCC gave you."

"Best couple hundred thousand dollars I ever spent," Trudy said. There hadn't been any more beer in her fridge, but there were a bunch of butter packets left over from the last time she'd gotten fast food. She peeled the foil off several and popped them in her mouth. Axton stared for a second but didn't bother asking.

"So no, Mr. Irving would know better than to expect you to put your name on any of his products. Not that your name is worth anything these days."

"You know, insulting me's probably not the best way to get me to agree to whatever the hell it is you're here for."

"It's not an insult. It's the truth. You know it is. If you didn't, you wouldn't be hiding in your condo drinking yourself into a stupor."

Trudy mashed a pat of butter into her mouth and sucked on it, not saying anything.

"He didn't send me here to offer you a business venture. He sent me here to offer you a job."

"I don't need a job."

"Oh? So your extended leave of absence from the zoo isn't indefinite after all?"

Again, she said nothing, although this time it took some effort. These days, any mention of the Cooper Memorial Zoo was likely to send her into a blind rage.

"Or maybe you're relying on the royalties from all your books?" Axton again selected a book from her shelf, this time a large coffee-table book of photography. Trudy hadn't taken most of the photos in the book, but she'd written the text and most of the photos featured her and her dear friends. Axton followed her into the kitchen and set the book on the counter in front of her. *Hollis in the Virungas*, the title said in small, subtle lettering. The title had never actually mattered, after all. All that mattered was the picture on the cover, the one that had originally appeared as a cover on National Geographic Magazine and won the photographer a Pulitzer. "I checked their rankings on Amazon before I came here, by the way. A few of them are still selling respectably, I guess."

Trudy winced. "Did you read any of the reviews?"

Axton nodded. "Amazon has removed a number of the ones that are most blatantly abusive, of course. The ones containing thinly disguised wishes for your death, and things like that. But enough are still there. You should know there's still a few people defending you in the reviews' comments. There are still people who believe in what you've accomplished, regardless of what the news of you is nowadays.

"Those royalties will only take you so far, though," Axton continued. "And the Hollis-Nelson Foundation, well, that's supposed to be a non-profit. You can't be getting any money for that, am I right?"

Trudy glared at him. "I'm pretty sure you already know the answer."

"I do. Or at least Mr. Irving does. All he bothered to tell me is that your lawyers are doing a spectacular job keeping the lawsuit quiet. He also tells me that he doesn't believe you're involved in any of the wrongdoing. And if he believes it, I don't see any reason why I shouldn't."

"Okay, so you've made your point. You're right. What little money I have left is going to run out soon. But what does Irving care? Our spheres of interest aren't exactly anywhere close to each other."

"You'll be surprised, I'm sure. There's more overlap than you think. And something that Mr. Irving has had his eye on suddenly requires some a certain type of trained eye. An expert."

"An expert on what, exactly?"

"What do you think? The one and only thing that you know more about than anyone else living in the entire world." He tapped his finger on the cover of the book, indicating the photo's subject. "All he wants to do at first is talk to you. If you're not interested, he's fine with that. He doesn't want anyone involved that isn't passionate about it. And, despite recent public outcry at what you did—"

"I had no choice," Trudy protested.

"What you were forced to do, then. You're still the most vocal advocate for the cause. *Their* cause."

He pointed at the picture again, and Trudy found herself staring at it for the first time in years. It was a picture of her, nearly thirty years younger than she was now, back when she'd barely been more than a raw recruit in the Peace Corps. Her dark skin was covered in sweat and dirt, the inevitable result of crawling through the African rain forest and hiding in the underbrush for three weeks. But this had been the moment where all of that effort had paid off. Because she wasn't alone in the picture. In front of her, a young blackback mountain gorilla stared her down, his face an odd mixture between stand-offish-ness and curiosity. He had his hand out to her, and she to him, their fingers hanging in the air and close to touching, yet not, in an unintentional reenactment of the ceiling of the Sistine Chapel.

Kramer, she'd named him. Whatever name he might have had among his own kind, to her and rest of the world he'd been known as Kramer.

"Fine," Trudy said. "I'll meet with him. But no promises."

Axton smiled. "That's all he sent me to ask."

CHAPTER TWO
SELL YOUR SOUL

Trudy was not completely unaccustomed to wealth. Her notoriety, before everything had gone wrong, had been enough to ensure that she lived comfortably, even if she chose to live modestly as well. She'd spent too much time living in leaking tents mere miles away from war zones to take any enjoyment out of an extravagant lifestyle. But she'd been toasted at fine banquets and been the guest of the President himself, so blatant displays of wealth didn't surprise her.

What did surprise her, as she took a seat in Irving's office, was the *lack* of displays of wealth. Trudy had done a little more research on the man before coming to this meeting, and she knew damned well that he could afford far better than this meager, gray-walled room with an IKEA-built desk and outdated carpet. There were a few pictures on the wall to break up the monotony, and as she waited for her host to arrive, she got up and looked at them. Several appeared to be official promo photos of the cast of *Sell Your Soul*, complete with the famous devil-horned logo down in the corner. Out of the eight seasons the show had been on the air, Irving had been a Buyer on six. From what little Trudy remembered, this photo seemed to be the Buyers of season five. Irving was the only black person in the group. There was one white woman, and the rest were all old white men. The white men, of course, were in front, but that did nothing to obscure Irving, whose broad shoulders seemed to push away the others even from behind. He was a presence that couldn't be ignored, but that had nothing to do with his size. There was an air of calm dignity to him that the other Buyers didn't seem to have. The others Buyers had a vaguely shifty feel to them. Irving looked like the kind of guy you could make a hand-shake deal with over a backyard barbeque and be sure he stuck to his side of the bargain.

Many of the other photographs were of Irving with various celebrities. Here he stood beside super-models in Milan, there he was at an Oscar party shaking hands with that year's Best Actor winner. Most of these had been put on the walls haphazardly. It was only the ones directly behind his desk that had been arranged with any care, and the quality of their frames added to the feel that these were the ones that truly mattered to him. These were pictures of him with various rock and rap stars. He looked younger in all of them. This had been the beginning of his career, long before he had been a billion-dollar mogul and reality television star. His only business then had been a small security company, hiring itself out for cheap to music acts that either hadn't made it big yet or were on the downward slide from their fame. It was entirely possible that he would have still been there and only there if Irving hadn't been in the wrong place at the wrong time (or the right place at the right time, depending on how one looked at it) in the mid-nineties.

At the center of the picture display behind his desk was one frame larger than all the others: a gold record, *Two-Time Hustlin' Blues* by rapper Magic Mustapha. Trudy had read about that on Irving's Wikipedia page. Mustapha had given the record to Irving, saying it wouldn't have existed without him. Quite true, considering that, during the album's recording, Irving had taken a bullet meant for the rapper. According to urban legend, most likely untrue, the album's number one single even featured a sample of the original gunshot along with Irving's grunt of pain.

And that was it. That was the entire office of one of the richest men in the city, and likely among the one hundred richest in the country. No attempt at comfort, nothing more than the obligatory attempt to impress any guests. And here Trudy sat, waiting for him. She wanted to say she wasn't intimidated, especially since the environment was practically Spartan. But it was the minimalism of this man's main office that freaked her out the most. She'd been in the parlors of warlords and presidents and prime ministers, and all those rooms had in some way been meant to intimidate.

The message Irving seemed to be sending with this particular room was that he didn't need to intimidate. He knew damn well exactly how much money and power he had, and he knew how to use it.

Axton had led her up to the office about half an hour ago. He'd wanted to do it immediately after first speaking to her, but they had both decided it might be better to wait a day so that she could wash some of the funk and alcohol smell off of her. Not that she still wouldn't have taken a little nip before coming, except somewhere in her self-flagellating bender she had finished off all the booze in her apartment. She'd considered going out to get more, but after a great deal of mental effort, she kept herself from falling off her temporary wagon. While she didn't expect that someone like Irving would really have anything worth listening to, she still allowed herself a little hope that this might be the opportunity to reclaim a small part of her life. She kept that hope small, though, not letting it grow beyond the tiniest seedling. And if it all turned out to be nothing but bullshit, there was still a liquor store between here and home.

She didn't turn around when the door opened behind her. Trudy was busy sucking on a couple of ketchup packets she had brought from home, and while she didn't give a rat's ass whether or not Irving saw her doing this, she wasn't going to interrupt herself for anyone, billionaire or not.

"Ms. Hollis," Irving said in that gentle yet deep voice that had made him one of the most popular Buyers on the show. "I cannot tell you how much of an honor it is to finally…" He finally came around his desk and saw her nursing the ketchup packets. Trudy always found this to be telling moment when she met someone new. The most common reaction was for the person to be disproportionately scandalized, as though her habit was an unforgivable violation of the social order. Irving, however, only paused long enough to take in the detail before continuing. "…to finally meet you. I've long been a follower of your work."

While his reaction to the ketchup was uncommon, his words weren't. Trudy couldn't even begin to count the times in her life she'd heard that sentiment, and so often the words seemed empty. However, she hadn't heard them in some time now, so for the first time in months, she actually felt flattered.

"Thank you," Trudy said around a mouth full of ketchup. "I'm confused."

Irving again eyed the ketchup packet in her mouth, then the small stack she'd put in front of her. "Are you, now?"

"Your underling said something about offering me a job."

"I thought you might need one."

"Maybe I do, maybe I don't. But I don't have the slightest clue what you think I could do for you."

"You don't? Tell me, in your mind, if I offered some random person on the street a job, what do you think I would have them do?"

"Uh, I don't have the slightest clue. Anything? Everything?"

"Why do you say that?"

"I don't know. Maybe because you have your hands in a little bit of everything. There's no telling what kind of position you might need filled."

"I see. You think of me that way, but you can't imagine that any of my many projects and corporations would have a use for someone like you?"

Trudy was silent for several seconds, thinking that over. "So do you have some kind of pitch for me or something?"

"Or something," Irving said. He finally sat down in his chair. He was a very wide man, and the chair didn't seem to fit him well, but none of that was because he was overweight. He was, in fact, very fit, exactly as he had been back when he first earned himself the nickname The Bouncer.

"I have a proposition for you," Irving said.

"A, you would have to buy me dinner first, and B, you're not my type."

He stared at her unblinkingly.

"Uh, right. Sorry. I apologize in advance for anything and everything snarky or idiotic I might say. It's been... rough recently."

He nodded, a look of genuine understanding on his face. "The way you've been portrayed in the media is unfair."

Trudy looked away and didn't say anything.

"Did you want to talk about it?" Irving asked. The question surprised Trudy. This was the first time since the incident happened that anyone had bothered to ask her how she felt. Everybody else, from talking head pundits on the news channels to every asshole with a YouTube channel, had been too busy screaming their own opinions to the world to listen to a thing she might have to say. And she found that she did want to talk. She just wasn't sure if she was ready yet. Trudy had spent so much of the last couple of months in a bottle that, she suddenly realized, she hadn't even been able to process much of it herself.

"Not really," she said, although something deep inside her protested the lie. "It's done. You've seen the videos. They were all over the news and the internet. You've probably even seen the memes."

Irving snorted. "Yeah, people these days do like expressing themselves through memes when they don't actually have any words worth saying. Have you seen the one of me eating a sandwich?"

"That rings a vague bell."

"All I was doing was sitting at a table at an outdoor café and eating a sandwich. Some random person takes of picture of it with their smartphone, and all of a sudden it's all about how desperately I need to get laid. Something about the look on my face, I guess. You would not believe some of the dirty messages I get from completely random people referencing that. As though that one picture means they suddenly know everything inside me."

"Except they don't," Trudy said softly. "No one truly knows was going on inside your head."

"Hell, I don't even know what was going through my head at that time. I mean, I was eating a sandwich, for fuck's sake. Who really has intimate memories of that sort of thing?"

Trudy looked away again.

"Ah, I'm sorry," Irving said. "I'm sure your situation is different. Me eating a sandwich is different than you, uh, you…"

"Go ahead. You can say it. Me shooting an endangered gorilla that I had watched over since he was a baby."

"Yes."

Trudy sighed. "Great. We've gone down memory lane. We've expressed our disappointment at the shallowness of society. Did you have anything else to say, or can I finally leave?"

"You can leave whenever you want. No one's forcing you to stay here. But if you do leave, you'll miss out on an unbelievable opportunity."

"Is this the time where you make me a monetary offer? You try to buy my soul like you and your friends do on your show?"

For the first time since their meeting began, Irving frowned. "Okay, a couple of points. First, I really wish the network executives had come up with some other name for the show than that. It automatically portrays me like I'm some kind of devil. No one forces those people to come on *Sell Your Soul*, no one pokes them with a pitchfork until they tell us their dreams and business ideas, and no one forces them to sign in blood when they accept whatever financial deal we offer them."

"What about that one picture that made the rounds a couple of years ago?"

"That jackass cut open his own finger and smeared it on the contract of his own will. I was just as disgusted as anyone else. All he wanted was his fifteen minutes of fame, and he got it. The failure of his company after that was his own lazy fault."

"Okay, fine. No actual soul selling involved. Gotcha."

"Second, don't call the other Buyers my friends. I can't stand those fuckers."

This took Trudy by surprise. "Wait, really? All of you always look so buddy-buddy in the publicity photos."

"And that's all they are. Publicity photos. I will swear right here and now on a Bible that I'm not some devil in disguise. But some of those other ones? Let's just say, there's rumors among us of a few bribes to pay off some rather unfortunate witnesses."

"Do I even want to know?"

"Not if you don't want to testify in front of a grand jury someday. Trust me. Most of the other Buyers are leeches on society. They wouldn't know an altruistic act if their lives depended on it."

"And you would?"

"I try."

"That's not a part of your personality a lot of people hear about."

"That's on purpose. If someone advertises that they're trying to do good in the world, they're probably not doing the good deed for its own sake."

"So is that what this is? You getting me off my pathetic ass is your good deed for the day?"

"Oh no. Not at all. If all you really want to do with the rest of your life is drink yourself into a stupor, that's your own damned business. But I think you want to get back to who you once were, don't you? You want to make a difference again, too."

Trudy didn't answer. This time, at least, she didn't look away.

Irving must have taken that as some kind of sign. He stood up and opened a drawer in his desk to pull out a manila folder.

"I've got some things I want to show you." He opened the folder and spread the papers inside out on the desk in front of her. "I'm not going to give you any context to start with. Tell me what you see here."

"Paper hard copies," Trudy mused. "How very old school."

"I have some of the best digital security possible, but I'm still paranoid about this getting out before I want it to. See if you could tell me why."

Most of the papers in the folder were photographs, but the one on top was a map. She picked it up, instantly recognized the region, and almost put it down before giving it a second look. It showed the Virunga Mountain range, a series of volcanoes, some dead and some still very much alive. The Virungas were deep in the interior of Africa and claimed in part by three different countries: Uganda, Rwanda, and the Democratic Republic of the Congo. Trudy herself, along with her predecessors Dian Fossey and George Schaller, was a big part of the reason why Westerners even knew anything about the Virungas. They were, after all, the only place in the world where one could find the endangered mountain gorilla. A large part of Trudy's nearly sixty years had been spent in the rain forests of these mountains.

So the map would have been unnecessary for her except for a series of red marks that someone had made on it. Most of them were small red x's, one or two showing in Rwanda, a few more in the Congo, and the largest concentration right on the border of Uganda in the region of the Bwindi Impenetrable Forest National Park. Each of the x's was accompanied by a small number, and she noticed that together they formed a very loose circle, in which someone had drawn a smaller circle with a large question mark in it right on the border between Uganda and the DRC.

She set that aside and took up the first photo. It had a number one up in the corner, leading Trudy to assume it corresponded to the numbered x on the map. It was a long-distance shot of a mountain gorilla hunkering down in the brush. Trudy's expertise told her that this was a juvenile, just short of adult, although she couldn't be sure if the gorilla was male or female. To a human, there was nothing at that age that clearly distinguished sex among gorillas unless they were older. Trudy took a closer look to see that the gorilla was leaning down and doing something. It looked to her like it was disabling some poacher trap.

"Okay, interesting but nothing new," she said. "Certain gorilla groups have been seen dismantling traps for many years now."

"Take a look at the next picture," Irving said.

She did. It was marked with the same number and looked like it had been taken a few seconds after the first. In this one, the gorilla was moving away from the assumed trap. There was less brush covering her view here, allowing her to see that the gorilla was carrying things in its hands. In one there was a long, sharpened stick. In the other, there was a flat, wedge-shaped rock.

She stared at this one for a lot longer. "Again, nothing new," she said, although she said it much slower, with less certainty. She looked up at Irving to see that he had arched an eyebrow at her. He knew as well as she did that there was indeed something unusual in this picture. The gorilla hadn't just found a way to disable a trap. It had used tools. This by itself was not the surprising thing. While it had once been treated as something unique among humans, many animals in nature had since been recorded using other objects to help them obtain their goals, gorillas included. But these tools were always found objects, simple sticks or stones or detritus left behind by humans.

It was possible that the stone the gorilla held had been found that way, even if it did look suspiciously like it had been chipped away into knife-like tool. The stick, on the other hand. There was no way that stick had gotten that way just by the gorilla breaking it off a branch. Someone had deliberately sharpened it.

Trudy looked up at Irving, starting to understand why this might be something of importance. The science media loved to pull out the old chestnut from time to time that various apes had entered the Stone Age, but there was a huge difference between using found tools and making their own.

"That picture doesn't really prove anything, though," Trudy said. "The forests around the Virungas aren't as pristine as Westerners like to believe. Humans have been coming and going through there for ages, and the farmlands go right up to the edge of the forest. This gorilla probably just found things that someone else had already made."

"Sure," Irving said. "But why don't you keep looking?"

Trudy flipped through a number of the photos, pausing on each only long enough to identify that many were similar. The majority of the pictures showed the remains of gorilla night nests, the small and simple structures gorillas built every night to sleep in. Most of them, as was common with gorillas, had feces sitting in the bottom. As horrifying as it might be to humans, gorillas thought nothing of defecating where they slept. But alongside many of the nests were more simple tools—sharpened sticks, shaped rocks, and, in one instance that made Trudy do a double-take, a short but thick branch with a wide, flat stone at the end that had been tied together with a dried vine. It didn't quite look like an ax, but it had obviously been made with some similar purpose.

Trudy stopped and stared at that ax-like object. She had dedicated her entire life to the study of mountain gorillas. It was unlikely that anyone currently alive knew more about them than she did. And despite their beautiful intelligence, despite their complex brains and social behaviors and patterns, Trudy knew, she absolutely *knew*, that a gorilla couldn't have made this. Unless...

"This isn't behavior they've spontaneously learned by themselves," Trudy said. "It's too much too quick. Someone must have taught them, trained them."

"That's what others have told me," Irving said. "The obvious question, then, is who."

"It shouldn't be any official ranger or guide in any of the parks around the Virungas," Trudy said. "The general policy these days is supposed to be nothing more than observing from a distance, especially since gorillas can get sick from human diseases and have no defenses against them."

Irving gestured at the photos. "There's still a few more. If you think you've seen all there is, you're in for a shock."

Trudy took a deep breath before flipping to the next photo. She'd expected another tool of some sort. Instead, she got something so different that it took her several seconds of staring before it started to register.

"It's a stack of rocks," Trudy said in a monotone voice.

"You know it's not."

She nodded her head. It wasn't a stack at all, in fact, but six distinct stones, five in a rough circle on the outside and one in the middle. Four of the outer five were roughly the same shape and size, about the size of a small potato standing on end, with one smaller. The outsides of the stones had been chipped away so that, if she squinted, she could almost believe they were intended to be rough approximations of gorillas themselves. The one in the center was similar yet also three times the size of the others.

She thought of the stone she had seen in the gorilla's hand in the second picture, of the strange tool sitting in the night nest. Judging from the way these six stones were chipped into their rough shapes, Trudy could imagine that those tools had been used to make these.

Art, Trudy realized. These gorillas were making art.

"This is a hoax," she said.

"Is it?" Irving asked, his tone making it clear that this was not just a rhetorical question. This was why she was here, she realized. Irving wanted to know if this was for real.

"It... it has to be."

"Haven't gorillas been known to make art before? What about Koko?"

"Koko's different," Trudy said. Everyone always had to bring up the famous gorilla Koko, and it annoyed her. "Koko was raised from a baby by humans. She was socialized like a human. Yes, she can speak sign language. Yes, she's been known to paint. But that's completely different than what gorillas in the wild naturally are inclined to do. Comparing Koko to the wild Virunga mountain gorillas is like comparing a pampered rich white dude to an uncontacted tribe in the Amazon. Just because they're the same species doesn't mean they have any context to understand each other's culture."

"And do wild mountain gorillas have that?"

"Have what?"

"Culture."

Trudy opened her mouth to speak, but she couldn't think of anything to say. Mountain gorillas were intelligent. They had rituals. They had something akin to language. Beyond that, they were different enough from humans that it wasn't fair to say what they did and didn't have. They certainly didn't have a culture in the way most humans would understand it, but that didn't mean it didn't exist. Just like her own example, humans might just not have the context to understand it.

"Okay, so maybe these gorillas have been making art. They've been making something. But are we sure it's them and not someone trying to pull an elaborate hoax?"

"Skip ahead to the last picture and you'll see. Don't lose your place, though. The most important pictures are yet to come."

Trudy pulled the picture from the bottom of the stack. Here was another photo that had been taken from a distance, but the angle on it allowed her to see better what the gorilla was doing. Just like in the other photos, there was one rock in the center. Two more were on the far side while a gorilla seemed to be setting up a third one, with two others sitting by its side.

"I guess that answers that question," Trudy said as she started to set the photo aside.

"Wait," Irving said. "You might want to take a closer look at that one."

She frowned but did what he asked. Was there something here she was missing? The stones looked nearly identical to one of the other pictures, enough that Trudy thought one of them might have been taken of the gorilla's handiwork after it had left. The gorilla itself was a good-sized specimen, obviously a fully matured male, as evidenced by the silver fur all down the saddle of his back. The gorilla was turned just enough to the camera that she could see his nose, and...

She gave an audible gasp.

"See, I thought that would interest you," Irving said.

"How do I know this isn't photoshopped?"

"You don't, but do you really suppose I would go to all this trouble just to prank you?"

Trudy supposed not, but she couldn't see how the picture could possibly be real. To anyone else in the world, this would just be a picture of a random gorilla. They couldn't tell one from the other. What the average person didn't know, though, was that each and every gorilla had a distinct "nose print," with slight inconsistencies in the nose's shape that allowed researchers to identify specific animals.

This nose print had a distinct diagonal scar on it running from the center and up to the right. Trudy knew that nose print. She'd better, considering she'd been photographed with it for the most famous gorilla picture in the world. This was Kramer, the exact same gorilla from the cover of *Hollis in the Virungas*.

"This can't be him," Trudy said. "He's dead. He was killed by poachers."

"According to your own writings, you never found a body."

"No, just massive amounts of blood and the headless bodies of several others in his group."

"So couldn't that be him?"

"I… I suppose." She stared at the photo with an unexpected ache in her heart. She'd sobbed for nearly a week at his death. All the gorillas in his group had been special to her, but Kramer more than the rest. In as much as it had been possible across species lines, Trudy had considered Kramer to be her friend.

"Is this why you wanted to bring me in on this?" Trudy asked.

"Yes," Irving said. "I had some of my people looking into tourism in a number of foreign countries with a special eye for conservation. I figured there was a way to make money and make the world a better place at the same time. And while they were looking, they found all the evidence you've seen here. I know that you're persona non grata right now to pretty much anyone with an internet connection, but I figured that if there was anyone who would best be able to look into this, maybe even who had the most *right* to look into this, it would be you."

Trudy wanted to thank him, but a lump formed in her throat before she could say anything. The right, he'd said. In Trudy's mind, after what she had done, she didn't have any right at all to continue working with these massive creatures. The drunken exile she'd put herself in was more than just self-pity and preservation against the death threats. It was her penance, and personally, she didn't think she'd finished paying it.

"I… I haven't done field work in a very long time," Trudy said. "I'm getting too old for it. Kramer deserves someone younger, someone with the energy to investigate this the way it should be. I'm not your woman."

"Even if it was a matter of life or death?" Irving asked.

"What do you mean?"

"The final photos. Take a look at them."

As Trudy took out the last set of photos, Irving kept talking. "Everything else you've seen so far is weird enough, according to the people I've already had working on it. But if that were all, they would have simply published some papers that would have been taken out of context in the science media for a couple weeks and then forgotten. But instead, we've been doing everything we can to keep a lid on it. Because of that."

She spread out the last several pictures in front of her. Trudy stared at them for several seconds, unsure of how she was supposed to respond to this, before finally managing, "I don't even know what I'm looking at."

"No? Maybe I can help. This over here is a severed head. In this picture over we have, uh, I'm not actually sure if that used to be an arm or a leg…"

"Not funny," Trudy said.

"No, it isn't. So please, take a very close look at these and tell me everything you see."

Trudy took a deep breath and forced herself to examine all the grizzly details. There were four photos, all of them taken out in the forest. Judging from the moisture, she guessed there'd recently been a heavy rain. This hadn't done much to wash away the blood, or else there had originally been so much blood that it couldn't be washed away so quickly.

"Poachers," she said, looking at the clothing of the three (or at least she thought it was three) men lying in multiple pieces around the murder site. That it was a murder of some kind wasn't even in doubt. "Although I don't see any weapons. Most poachers I tended to run into were usually armed."

"Good eye. My contact in the field didn't even notice that right away. What else?"

"The brush around them is severely trampled. Given that, my initial guess would have been that they'd been trampled by a stampeding herd of Cape buffalo."

"But?"

"But then they would just be crushed. It looks more like someone took a machete to these men and then gleefully flung the parts around."

"Does it really?"

Something about the way Irving said that caused Trudy to take a closer look at one of the photos of a severed arm. "No. I guess you're right. Even a dull machete would have left a cleaner wound than that. It's almost like..." She stopped and looked up at him. "No."

"Yes," Irving said.

"No. That can't be right. You can't be about to tell me that gorillas did this."

"Could they, though?"

"I... no. I don't think so? I mean, an adult silverback might have the strength for it, but no gorilla ever in recorded history has shown that level of ferocity. I've lived among them for most of my life. Almost always, when they look aggressive, it's just a way to scare others away from their... territory..."

She trailed off, as she was getting far too close to recent events. That was what the digital lynch mobs of social media had tried saying about what happened between her and Killroy. Plenty of fellow experts in the field had come to her defense, saying that yes, a gorilla could be that dangerous under the right circumstances, but the public hadn't wanted to hear that. And now, whether she'd intended to or not, she was agreeing with them.

Irving nodded at her obvious discomfort. "I know what you're thinking, and we don't have to go there. Let me make this easier for you. Look at the photos again. Look at the track."

She did look, although she didn't see any gorilla tracks. There were some fibers here or that that might have been gorilla fur, but beyond that, she couldn't see anything at all that even suggested gorillas had done this. Trudy spread the pictures out, looking again. The first three were closer shots of the bodies, or at least what was left of them. The fourth shot was a wide angle of the whole scene, including the flattened vegetation around them, and…

Holy shit.

Irving hadn't said tracks, as in multiple gorillas or even multiple feet.

He'd said track. Singular.

"Now you see it. Now you understand why we want to keep this quiet for the moment, and why I want you, the world's leading gorilla expert, taking point on this from now on."

"This can't be real," Trudy said. "This is a hoax."

"If it is, you'd be the one who could prove it. So what do you say? Will you work for me on this? Find out everything you can about what the hell is going on in the Virungas. I will pay for everything. I will completely outfit you. I will even do everything I can to grease the wheels of diplomacy if you need to cross between the three countries."

"And what do you get out of it in the end?"

"I get the bragging rights of having the foresight to fund all this. I can buy anything I want at this point, Miss Hollis. It gets boring. But going down with you in history and science books? Not boring at all."

Trudy tried to pull her eyes away from the final photo. The rain had worn away the distinct edges of the crumpled brush, but now she knew why so much of the blood hadn't washed away. It was in the middle of a depression. The poachers had been ripped apart, then trampled.

By a single, wide object. There was no way to be certain, but it looked like a gigantic gorilla footprint.

"When do I leave?" Trudy asked.

CHAPTER THREE:
STRANGE BEDFELLOWS

Hollis-Nelson. Trudy tried not to make any audible noise of frustration at the name on the sign the driver held up as he waited for her at the Entebbe International Airport in Kampala, Uganda. Her divorce from the Nelson half of her name had been even before her entire life had taken its turn toward pear-shaped. And yet that name continued to haunt her just as much as the name Killroy.

"That's me," Trudy said to the driver in Luganda. She probably could have spoken English, but she had gone so long since exercising her linguistic skills that she couldn't help herself.

The driver looked surprised at her. "You cannot be Miss Hollis-Nelson," he said in heavily accented English. Trudy responded in kind.

"Were you expecting something else?"

"Uh, yes. I thought you would be a *muzunga.*" *Muzunga.* A white foreigner. Of course, for anyone who didn't know her name, they would assume a scientific expert from America would be white.

"Well, I'm not."

"No matter. The other one is, at least."

He led her out the door to a car. Although it wasn't anything fancy, it was still practically new, which put it ahead of many of the other vehicles zooming around in the street.

"What other one?" Trudy asked.

"The other person hired by Mr. Irving. She will meet you at the hotel, I am told."

Other person. There were many other people Irving could have hired to help her with this expedition. Trudy, however, suddenly thought of one specific person. "Is it a man or a woman?"

"A woman." He paused as if not sure he should say anything else, then added, "Very large," holding his hands out in front of his chest.

Oh hell. It couldn't be. There could have been any number of white women with ample chests under Irving's employ. But only one specific one came to Trudy's mind.

It's not her. It can't be her. Please don't let it be her. This whole situation is already awkward and dangerous enough.

The driver chattered at her the entire time he drove, which was quite the amount of time in the typical Kampala traffic. Trudy tried to keep one ear open to everything he said, although for most of the time she zoned out in a weird sense of nostalgia. Uganda, Rwanda, and the Democratic Republic of the Congo. Three countries she had known intimately before she had gone into semi-retirement as a part of the Cooper Memorial Zoo. These places would never be her home, especially since countries like Uganda had actual laws against people like Trudy being themselves. But she knew and respected much of the culture. And it was a world the average American would never see, nor even make the slightest attempt to understand.

The driver let her out at her hotel. It was Trudy's understanding that she wouldn't be in the hotel for long at all, just long enough for the whole expedition team to get together and then head off to the southwest in the direction of the Virungas. The hotel was the fanciest available in Kampala, again thanks to Irving's influence. Personally, even at the height of her international fame, Trudy had never stayed in any place like this. She'd preferred the smaller, homier places, the places where she could go to the makeshift bar next door and get the homemade pineapple or banana moonshine that the majority of the population drank when they wanted to get drunk and kill a few brain cells. She wasn't going to complain about her lodgings this time, though. After being treated for weeks like the worst human being on the planet by everyone with a Wi-Fi connection, she thought she could take just a little bit of the royal treatment.

She walked in the door and started toward the desk. Before

she could even ask about her room, though, a voice came from behind her.

"Don't bother to ask. Our whole team's got a suite together for tonight and tomorrow, so you can just follow me up."

Trudy stopped and closed her eyes, knowing exactly who she would see when she opened them.

Aw shit. It really is her. Just look her in the eye and pretend you don't remember anything. Don't think about that night at Karisoke. Don't think about the way her hair looked on the pillow. And for the love of God, don't think about that mole on the inner side of her left breast where, if you touch it...

"Trudy? Are you okay?"

Trudy opened her eyes. Gerta Lyndholme herself stood before her, looking somehow curious, playful, and worried all at the same time. The white woman hadn't changed much in the over ten years since they'd last seen each other. There were a few more wrinkles on her delicate Austrian features, and her clothing here in the hotel was more conservative than what Trudy had gotten used to in the field. But otherwise, there was no mistaking her for a different person. This was the same woman she'd shared a bed with last time she'd been in the Virungas.

"I'm... fine. I wasn't expecting you."

"Irving didn't tell you that I was the one working as his current contact in the field, did he?"

"No, he must have let that little bit of information slip his mind. He must not have known that we have a history." She made sure to keep her voice low as she said this, so no one else in the hotel lobby might get the idea that they were more than just teammates. Homosexuality was illegal in Uganda. If anyone caught the two of them together, it could mean a life in prison.

"Oh, he knew. I asked him not to say anything. I was afraid you might not come if you knew I was a part of the group."

"What, are you trying to trick me back into your bed?"

Gerta frowned and looked genuinely hurt. "I would never trick you. I just thought that, with you being married now and all, you might decide to set aside the biggest-ever discovery in primatology just because you were afraid of the awkwardness."

"Uh, you do know I'm not married anymore, right?" Trudy

asked.

"No, I didn't. I'm sorry. I guess I'm just making the awkwardness worse."

Trudy looked around again to make sure they didn't have an audience. "Look," she whispered. "We're both adults. We can handle this like adults. Do you want to just get the awkwardness out of the way so we get going on the science already?"

Gerta raised an eyebrow.

Forty-five minutes later, Trudy stretched her naked form out on Gerta's bed in the penthouse suite. Gerta stood up to get a towel to wipe down the sweat and other fluids they had accumulated on the bed. When she came back, she took Trudy by the chin, and they both looked each other sleepily in the eyes.

"So are we good?" Gerta asked softly.

"I am if you are."

"Because you this can't happen in the field where others can see us."

"I know. It's out of my system now," Trudy said. A complicated look went over Gerta's face, part disbelief that Trudy could possibly be finished with this and part hurt that maybe Trudy might actually be telling the truth. Trudy, for her part, couldn't say whether she was being truthful or not. She'd been wound so tight lately, and now, for the first time in over a month, she wasn't. She had to admit that she probably wasn't thinking clearly. All the more reason to be done with the loveplay for now and get down to business.

To emphasize this, Trudy leaned over the bed and grabbed her bra from where she'd carelessly tossed it. Still languid and sleepy, she had trouble with the hooks behind her back. Gerta knelt on the bed behind her and did the clasps for her. There was nothing sexual about the touch now. Just two colleagues helping each other out.

"So if you're Irving's woman in the field, does that mean you can fill me in on all the details Irving was too clandestine to give me?"

"I can try. Any actual scientific data we have so far is minimal, so most of what I can give you is conjecture. Here, now that I've done you, you do me." She turned around and let Trudy help her with her own lemon-yellow bra. "So ask away."

"What exactly are we dealing with here?"

"Too broad of a question. Not sure I can give a good answer yet. Narrow it down."

Trudy went over the file Irving had shown her in her mind. Although there were many bits of weirdness among it all, her heart commanded her to immediately gravitate to one specific mystery.

"Tell me about Kramer."

"So it is Kramer then?" Gerta asked. "You're sure?"

"I know that nose print anywhere. He was..." She hesitated, knowing what kind of looks her next words would have gotten her in the States. But here in Uganda, with a dedicated colleague by her side, she knew at least she wouldn't get laughed at. "He was my friend. So yeah, I recognized him."

"Then I don't need to tell you the shock I felt when I took that picture and suspected who it was. One of the most famous gorillas in the world, murdered years ago, still alive."

Trudy didn't say anything as Gerta called Kramer's supposed death a murder. She expected Gerta to segue into a question about what had happened that fateful day at the zoo, but the question never came. Maybe, this far from America, the news about what had happened and what Trudy had done either hadn't made it this far or was treated like a non-issue.

Instead, she gave Trudy a quick peck on the shoulder before searching the mess they'd left on the floor for her underwear. "I'm sure you want as much information about Kramer as possible right now, but I'm sorry to say..."

"You know what? Let's not talk about Kramer," Trudy said. Gerta stopped what she was doing and gave Trudy a look like she had spontaneously grown a third leg.

"You don't want to talk about him? After everything you went through when you thought he was dead..."

"No, look, we can talk about everything all at once when we're with the rest of the team. There is a lot more to the team, I'm assuming?"

"Um, yes. They should be arriving over the next couple of hours. But if you don't want to talk about Kramer, then..."

"Let's talk about you," Trudy said.

"Are you deflecting from something?"

"Yes."

Gerta smiled. "At least you are honest. Fine then. Talk about me. What do you want to know?"

"Well, for starters, why are you even here? You definitely can't still be with the Peace Corps after all this time."

"No, you are right. I did my three-year term of service with them, and then as they usually suggest, I left, not trying to stay, and eventually turning all the good I tried to do sour. But here's the thing. When you spend years helping locals establish a gorilla tourist trade, you become known in some circles as a gorilla expert. And when people can't afford someone like the great Trudy Hollis, then have to go for the low-rent version. Like me."

The way she talked made Trudy even more painfully aware that Gerta had no idea about Trudy's fall from grace. She wondered how long she could keep it that way. Or if she even should.

Trudy put on her own underwear as Gerta continued. "So I went back to Austria for a bit, continued my education, then ended up back in the Rwanda and Uganda area for a time. Then, when Uganda's "Kill the Gays" law was at its height, I got the hell out of here and worked with the lowland gorillas in Gabon for a time. I said at the time that no one would be able to pay me to come back to a place where they'd ever considered putting people like us to death, but to be honest, there are a lot of other countries with laws almost as bad. My choice was either giving up working with gorillas altogether, or else getting really good at hiding my sexuality in public. And then, of course, Irving came along and proved that I *could* be paid enough to come back here."

"But what is his interest even in gorillas?" Trudy asked. "There's nothing about him that would make me think he would be a conservationist."

"Yes, I hear he is on a reality show now, or something like that? I do not pay that much attention to the American media. But he has put a lot of money into many things in this region. Improving schools, encouraging eco-tourism and conservation. I guess there just comes a point where a person gets bored buying yet another Ferrari."

As Trudy bent down to put on her pants, she felt Gerta's presence behind her, her hips close against Trudy's legs and, as Trudy stood straight, Gerta's breasts against her back. She thought for a second that Gerta was about to tear off her clothes again and begin a second round of lovemaking, but instead, all she did was lightly put her hands on Trudy's shoulders and whisper in her ear.

"I'm not going to ask how you're doing, but if you want to talk, I'm here."

Trudy turned to look at her, but the woman had already gone and vanished into the bathroom.

Dear God, what am I doing with her again? Trudy wondered to herself. It had been over ten years since they had last seen each other. They had technically never broken up, since they had never gone so far as to define themselves as being together in the first place. They had exactly two things in common: that they loved the wild, and that they were both lesbians. Beyond that, there was nothing. Trudy had grown up with a middle-class family in a huge city. Gerta had lived with her poor grandmother on a run-down farm. Gerta was cool and gentle at almost all times, whereas Trudy could run hot and lose herself easily to booze and her temper. They weren't even anywhere close to each other in age. With a twenty-three-year age difference, Trudy could have literally been Gerta's mother.

And yet, despite all this, the very first thing they had done after not seeing each other for a decade was fall into bed together again.

Already this expedition was far more than she had bargained for, and Trudy hadn't even been in Uganda for a full day. She wanted to grab a bottle of scotch and crawl back into bed, forgetting all the promises she had made to Irving.

She couldn't, though. Kramer was out there.

Gerta came out of the bathroom completely dressed in a stained but otherwise intact Charlie's Angels T-shirt that she had probably gotten second hand somewhere here in Kampala. She tied her long brown hair back in a loose ponytail as Trudy buttoned up her own shirt.

"Soooo… I'm assuming that means you do know all that's been going on with me."

"I'm sorry I missed the detail about your divorce, but just because this is Uganda doesn't mean it's backwards, Trudy. We have internet. We have Facebook. I wouldn't say that means I know what's going on with you, though. It just means I know what all the internet trolls are saying is going on with you."

"Just let me explain…"

"You don't need to explain. If you ever need to *talk*, though, I'm here."

Trudy stared at her through slit eyes. This was simply the way Gerta was, but Trudy couldn't help but feel a natural distrust at that much empathy and understanding. She had lived for well over half a century now, and she had seen murders, brutal violence, and lynch mobs both figurative and literal. As much as she desperately wanted to believe that someone stood in front of her that really cared, Trudy's naturally built-up paranoia wanted her to believe that she couldn't say what had happened that day with Killroy. Not what had *really* happened. Because for all the horrible things that the public said about her, she knew in her heart that the truth was far worse.

Jesus, she really needed some liquor about now.

From somewhere else in the suite, Trudy could hear a door open.

"Shit, that must be the rest of the group," Gerta said, suddenly rushing to hide any sign that she and Trudy had been doing anything more than talking this whole time.

"I thought you said it would be a while yet?" Trudy hissed as she tried to put her pants on, then realized as they were halfway up her legs that they were backwards.

"Yeah, well, I was counting on the traffic. It must have hit one of those rare moments where it spontaneously got better."

"Mrs. Lyndholme? Are you in here?" Trudy recognized the voice as Axton only seconds before he appeared in the bedroom doorway. Not expecting visitors, they hadn't bothered to close it. Axton stopped just inside the door, saw Trudy still buttoning her clothes, looked at Gerta trying to make the bed, and then turned around and walked back out without a further word.

Trudy stood in stunned silence, the belt on her pants still undone. There were a number of things that had just happened that she wanted to address, yet she didn't have the slightest clue where to start.

Gerta saw the way Trudy looked and answered at least one of the questions she had. "Uh, you didn't know that Axton and Irving were both coming with us on the expedition, did you?"

Trudy slowly shook her head.

"Look, I know they don't seem like the first choices we would want for something like this, but Irving's funding us, so I'm sure you agree that, if he and his assistant want to be a part of this, they have that right."

"Sure," Trudy mumbled. Gerta, now fully dressed, moved to give Trudy a quick peck on the lips, but Trudy backed away.

"What?" Gerta asked. "Axton and Irving already know that we're not straight, and they know what the laws are here. We won't have to worry about them outing us while we're in Uganda."

"Gerta," Trudy said softly.

"What?"

"He called you 'Mrs.'"

"Oh. Ohhhhh," she said, backing away from Trudy with her cheeks flushing pink. "Right. Um, there's something I forgot to tell you. I'm married."

CHAPTER FOUR:
THE MEDIOCRE SEVEN

"You forgot? You just up and forgot? Jesus fucking wept, Gerta, how the hell do you just forget you're married when you're in bed with someone else?"

"Okay, look. I see you're upset. Just..."

"Upset? Of course I'm upset. I just helped you cheat! I'm the other woman! I'm just like..." Trudy couldn't say the woman's name. Ever since her wife had divorced her to be with another woman, she'd actively refused to say it. The other woman, in her mind, didn't even deserve a name. And now here she was, acting as that other woman.

"Okay, Trudy? You're starting to hyperventilate. Take deep breaths." Gerta reached out to take Trudy by the shoulders, but Trudy backed away, hitting the bed with her calves and almost falling over.

"Don't touch me!" Trudy said.

"Just let me explain..."

"No, there's nothing you can say that..."

"Trudy, it's not real!"

Trudy stopped talking.

"Okay, are you done? We can talk about it soon, but right now, we have other people with us. We should probably have this conversation when they aren't around."

"Fine, but just give me a little more explanation first. What do you mean, it's not real? You mean your marriage?"

"Well, it's real enough legally, I guess. But Arnold and I, we are what you Americans call... I want to say that the term is that we are moustaches?"

Trudy frowned and thought that over. "Do you mean beards?"

"Yes, I suppose so. Our marriage is a sham. So you and I didn't do anything wrong. Can we just leave it at that until later?"

"I suppose."

"Good. I will go say hello to Axton and Irving. You stay in here and get yourself together, okay? You look freaked out."

"Right. Sure."

Gerta left the room. Trudy sat down on the bed and processed this. Okay, so, big deal, right? The woman she had just slept with for the first time in a decade was married, but it was apparently a marriage that didn't mean anything. Or that was what Trudy thought. She would need to ask Gerta for more details to make sure that what Trudy thought was what Gerta meant. She could be interpreting the term beard differently. In the slang Trudy was familiar with, a "beard" was someone that a gay or lesbian person was with to help them appear as though they were straight. She supposed that made sense, especially since Gerta spent more times in countries that were less accepting that she was a lesbian.

Still, although that seemed logical enough, Trudy felt hurt, and it surprised her. Gerta didn't actually mean anything to her, or at least she wasn't supposed to. Trudy hadn't even thought of her in years.

No, that wasn't true, she realized. She'd actually been thinking about Gerta a lot, especially after her divorce. Seeing Gerta again had ignited a tiny spark that Trudy thought had gone out completely.

Still, she knew before that nothing could come of it, and this new knowledge only reinforced that.

Right, Trudy thought. *Just keep telling yourself that, and eventually, you'll believe it.*

When she finally came out of the bedroom, she found Gerta, Irving, and Axton all sitting around a table. Gerta chatted idly with Irving, while Axton, obviously still embarrassed, wouldn't meet either Trudy or Gerta's eyes.

"Hollis, I'm so glad you made it here okay," Irving said as he stood up from the table to shake her hand. With absolutely no trace of irony in his voice, he said, "I see that you've already gotten acquainted with Gerta."

"Um, yes."

Gerta smiled at her. "You don't need to be coy. He's just joking around. I'm the one who lobbied so hard to get him to make you an offer. He already knows that we have… a history."

Trudy raised an eyebrow at Irving. "And are you aware that it's a history that could get us thrown in prison in this country?"

"You'll both be perfectly safe. I guarantee it."

Trudy was sure that he was right and his influence would keep any authorities off of them should she and Gerta need to have any more dalliances, but she deeply disliked the way he casually dismissed the concern. Just because they were under the protection of an American billionaire, that didn't mean that these horrid laws weren't used to imprison uncountable LGBTQ people in Uganda every day. But it wasn't Irving's country, so he probably didn't feel any special urge to care.

"I wasn't aware that you had any interest in being part of the expedition," Trudy said to him.

"There's a lot of things about me that people aren't aware of."

"And you know that this isn't going to be a simple walk in the park? Although I guess that's literally what we're going to be doing."

Axton finally looked at her. "It was my understanding that Bwindi Impenetrable Forest is more of a tourist site than an actual wilderness. Is that not right?"

"Yes and no," Gerta said.

"We're certainly not going to be visiting the same Virunga volcanoes that were around when Dian Fossey first started bringing global attention to the region," Trudy said. "The awareness she helped bring before she died eventually led to a rise in eco-tourism, especially during the nineties. We're not going into uncharted terrain like the white European explorers that jabbed their flags all around this region in old times. But there's a big difference between this kind of tourist destination and something like, say, the National Mall in D.C. or Times Square. You're going to have to work to get to where we're going. And speaking of which, I'm still not one hundred percent certain where exactly we intend to go. Or even what your final plans for this whole thing are, Irving."

"I don't have final plans yet. This is purely exploratory.

Something extraordinary is going on out there, and I want to be a part of revealing it to the world."

"What, so you can invest in tourism?"

"I wouldn't be adverse to it, but honestly, Trudy, I wish you would think higher of me. I'm just as much motivated by curiosity about the natural world as you are."

Trudy looked him up and down and thought she finally understood. He was getting older, although he was still just short of a decade younger than Trudy herself. This was almost like some kind of mid-life crisis with him. He was tired of the reality show cameras and corporate boardrooms. He wanted a good, old-fashioned adventure.

Well, she couldn't really blame him for that. That was why Gerta and Trudy had both started, after all.

"And him?" Trudy asked, pointing at Axton.

"He's here to help," Irving said. "Wherever I go, he goes."

"Couldn't get me to leave his side if you tried," Axton said with decidedly less enthusiasm than his employer.

"Is this supposed to be the entire team, then?" Trudy asked. "Because if it is, I have to say, I don't think this was planned very well."

"Please give me some credit, Trudy," Gerta said. "I am not a novice at planning these kinds of things. I have two trackers I trust very well that will meet us at the edge of Bwindi. You've probably even heard of them. Big Isaiah and Medium Isaiah."

Trudy nodded. They'd been working as trackers in that region for a long time, even if they had started after Trudy had gone into her semi-retirement. Some of Trudy's other colleagues spoke highly of them.

"Uh, is there a little Isaiah?" Axton asked.

"There was," Gerta said, "but he grew bigger than his brother, so it no longer felt right to call him little. That's when he started going by Medium Isaiah."

"Well, if he's bigger than his brother, then why isn't he Big Isaiah?"

"Because Big Isaiah is already Big Isaiah. I wouldn't ask them about any of that, though. It is a guaranteed way to start a spat."

"So it's the six of us, then?" Trudy asked.

Gerta frowned. "No, I was told there would be one more, but Mr. Irving has not been forthcoming with this last person's name."

"Yes, well, the seventh member of our team will also meet us at Bwindi. I suppose I better prepare you for him before we go. Before I say anything else, I need to remind you both that you already signed a contract, and that backing out of the expedition now for anything other than medical emergencies would result in you being forced to pay a significant penalty fee."

"I do not like the sound of this," Gerta said.

"Yeah," Trudy said. "Is this the part where we find out that we sold our soul to Irving the Buyer after all?"

"Well, I'm not the one who's going to be concerned about your soul. That's going to be our seventh member. Before I explain him, though, I want us to go over everything we know so far."

Axton pulled out the same file folder that Trudy had perused in Irving's office. He spread out the photos on the table, positioning the ones of the sculpted stones so they were the most prominent.

"So both of you," Irving said. "Tell me what you think these are."

"I already told you I don't think anything specific about them at all, other than that they're remarkable," Trudy said. "I want to wait until I see them in the wild, their placement, the little details of their workmanship. Hell, if we're lucky, we might even see some of the gorillas building them."

"And I think they are art," Gerta said. Trudy opened up her mouth to speak, but Gerta stopped her. "I already know what you are going to say. Artistic ideas do not typically arise in species or cultures that do not have time for them. The level of artistic aspirations a society has is based on the amount of their leisure time, and the dietary needs of gorillas mean that they do not have leisure time. They spend all their time foraging for enough nutrition to suit their needs. Is that about what you were going to say?"

"Uh, yeah, something more or less to that effect. How did you know?"

"I heard that exact same lecture from you many years ago."

"I don't recall ever telling you that."

"You lecture in your sleep."

Since Trudy couldn't be sure whether or not Gerta was kidding, she dropped it.

"But I feel like there is a flaw in that idea," Gerta continued. "Simply put, gorillas play."

"What does that have to do with anything?" Axton asked.

"Humans play, too, yet not all human play is physical. If we see young gorillas chasing each other in primitive games of tag, then I don't see how they can't also have similar ways of play that are not necessarily physical. The only thing they might lack for such an endeavor is the tools. And as we've already seen, tools are now somehow at their disposal."

"Yeah," Axton said. "In fact, I think I heard something about painting and that gorilla Koko…"

"Don't mention Koko," both Trudy and Gerta said at once. Axton held up his hands and backed away.

"So I guess you're trying to say that you think gorillas daydream?" Irving asked.

"Why not? Their brains have enough similarity to ours," Gerta said. "I admit, the better person to answer that question might be someone who has actually studied gorilla brains. They could maybe tell us if the corresponding parts of a gorilla brain are large or active enough to compare to whatever controls such things in a human brain."

"Ms. Hollis? You're the expert on gorillas and their biology. Do you think that's possible?"

"I've studied their habits and culture in the wild, Irving. I haven't gone around cutting open their heads."

"But surely some gorillas in captivity have been scanned in MRIs or something like that, right?"

"Well, there was extensive medical testing on… um, Killroy, to make sure he stayed healthy. But never a full scan of his brain. If such a thing has been done at other zoos, then, well, I guess I'm out of the loop. And I sure as hell wasn't welcome at Killroy's autopsy."

"Give me your guess, then, at least," Irving said. "Do gorillas daydream?"

Trudy thought back to the uncountable hours she had spent in the Virunga mountains, the times she had simply sat watching Kramer and the others in his group. They played, yes. They fought. They mated. They slept. They spent massive amounts of time foraging for foods nutritional enough to feed their hulking bodies. And sometimes, just sometimes, she would see Kramer sitting there, doing nothing but staring off into space, not bothering to brush away the insects crawling over his face. And she had wondered.

"Yes," Trudy finally said. "I definitely think it's possible. Even likely. There are things going on inside their heads that we couldn't possibly know."

"Couldn't possibly because we have no way of communicating?" Irving asked.

"Not really."

"And if they *did* make art in the wild? What would that tell you?"

"Well, I'm no psychology major, but isn't art the one thing that we really believe separates us from animals? We can and do express ourselves in ways that don't immediately benefit us in any way. If we saw animals in the wild doing that, then that might as well be the final barrier. Those animals would well and truly be just like us."

"And if they were just like us, might they share other traits that humans have?" Irving asked.

"I get the feeling that you're leading to something specific," Trudy said. "Why don't you just stop being cutesy and tell us already."

"Religion," Irving said. "Do you think gorillas could have religion?"

That took Trudy aback. "Uh, I suppose? I don't know. I've never really thought about it."

"Really, not even once in all your time in the field? What about you, Mrs. Lyndholme?"

"I admit I have been curious. I mean, when they look up at the sky, do they wonder what it is? When they see everything around them, do they wonder where it comes from?"

"Wait, wait, wait," Trudy said to Irving. "I think I see where you're going with this, and frankly, it's kind of crazy. These structures they're building, you think they're serving some kind of religious purpose? You don't think they're art at all?"

"No, I do think they're art. But how much of the great art in the world came about because of religion? The Sistine Chapel, *The Garden of Earthly Delights, the Last Supper…*"

Trudy raised an eyebrow. *"Why God No Give Me Hos?* by Magic Mustapha?"

Irving pointed an accusing finger at her. "Hey, I was just the bodyguard. I had nothing to do with that piece of garbage track. I told Magic it sucked, but he just had to release it anyway. Don't get off the subject."

"I don't know, that seems like a pretty big leap," Gerta said. "I'm looking, but I'm not sure that I see anything in these pictures that implies religion or worship."

"You don't? Maybe you should look again. You two may be the experts, but I did read your books, Ms. Hollis. I know that researchers in the field use nose prints to identify individual gorillas. Look at all the photos and tell me if you count the same number of unique mountain gorillas that I do."

Both Trudy and Gerta bent over the table and looked closely. Trudy was distracted for a moment by Gerta's proximity, especially the way her boobs pressed against the table and threatened to throw the photos underneath into dishevelment, but once her mind focused completely on the gorillas, there was nothing else in the world.

"Hmmm," Trudy said, checking the pictures versus where on the map they had been taken. "I'm seeing four distinct nose prints." She had a thought. Funny how easy it was to do that when there wasn't huge quantities of alcohol flowing through her system. "Kramer's is the only one I recognize off the top of my head, but I have most of my old notes digitized on my laptop. I can check to see if there are any other matches from the old days. Also, if I could somehow get copies of notes from any other researchers or tour guides in the area…"

Irving waved his hand dismissively. "Mrs. Lyndholme has most of the field research notes I was able to get from the area, but I'll keep my people on the lookout. Right now, though, I'm less concerned with whether or not they're familiar than I am with their numbers."

"I count four, too, although the radius of their pattern seems a little too big for the movement of a typical gorilla group," Gerta said. "Look here. See this gorilla right here? That's definitely the same one from this picture, but it was taken all the way over in this area." She pointed at a place on the map. "Gorillas don't usually go that far."

"I think we've already established that these gorillas are different," Irving said. "So, four. What are the chances that our people have caught pictures of every gorilla within this particular group?"

"Actually, I wouldn't say we can even be sure that it is one group," Trudy said. "Look, there's no more than one gorilla in each picture. Either your photographer was specifically trying to get shots of single gorillas, or they went out and did these things by themselves. Highly irregular. Gorilla groups stick together unless one of the members gets kicked out over dominance and politics. They wouldn't just break up and go do their own thing for a while."

"And considering I'm the photographer on most of these," Gerta said, "I can tell you that I wasn't cropping out anyone else."

"Interesting, but still beside the point," Irving said. "So this probably isn't all the gorillas involved. If you had to make a guess, how many would you say there probably are? Perhaps five?"

Trudy suddenly understood where he was going with this line of thought. "The circles of stone carvings. You think the five smaller stones represent the gorillas in this particular group."

Gerta sat up straight, blessedly pulling her ample bosom away from Trudy. "Which would mean you think the larger stone is supposed to represent their god."

Irving nodded. Although he tried to stay serious, he was obviously having a hard time containing his glee at the possible implications. "Meaning we would have here the first ever proven cult among creatures other than humans."

"Jesus," Trudy said. The ramifications of this possibility were astounding, but as a scientist, she had to temper her enthusiasm until they had proof. And right now, everything was pretty circumstantial. "Then what about the giant gorilla footprint?" she asked.

"Two possibilities that I see, unless you two can come up with more," Irving said. "One, the footprint is fake. And I don't mean some humans created it as a prank."

"Although we should definitely keep that in mind as a possibility," Trudy said.

"True enough. We'll wait for whatever evidence we might be able to find in the field. But when I say fake, I'm thinking that the gorillas themselves faked it, like they intentionally created a sign of the god they believe in."

"And the other possibility?" Gerta asked. The wide-eyed look she gave Trudy told her that Gerta already knew exactly what the other possibility was. It was far-fetched, and yet if they found proper evidence...

"Two, the footprint is real. The gorilla cult's god is real. It's an actual, honest-to-God, giant gorilla out of *King Kong* or *Godzilla*."

"Both possibilities are ridiculous," Trudy said.

"And yet..." Irving gestured at the picture of the footprint. "If either one holds any truth at all, it will be the greatest scientific and biological find since Darwin went to the Galápagos."

"Alright, so I see what you're cooking here," Trudy said. "This final person on our expedition. He or she is some sort of expert on religion. Am I right?"

Surprisingly, for the first time since Trudy had seen them together, Irving gave Axton a disapproving scowl. "I'll let my *assistant* tell you about that part." That he emphasized the word "assistant," Trudy had a guess that Axton was about to tell them about something that had almost cost him that cushy position.

Axton sighed. "Mr. Irving, I've already told you. I don't know where the leak came from, but it couldn't have come from me or anyone I hired."

"Just tell Ms. Hollis and Mrs. Lyndholme already. They're the ones who are going to be most put out by this."

Trudy and Gerta exchanged worried looks.

"As soon as Mr. Irving started wondering if religion might be a factor in what we're seeing," Axton said slowly, "I started to put out feelers for someone that might be able to act as an expert on the expedition."

"And?" Trudy asked.

"And someone else found out."

"Someone else?" Gerta asked. "Just any someone else? Because I'm starting to get nervous where this is going."

"And you have a right to be," Irving said softly. "Tell them, Axton."

"A certain person active in the region found out, and he said that if he wasn't allowed to be a part of the expedition as our religious expert, he would leak all the news we had. Fortune hunters of all shapes and sizes would descend on the Virungas and try to prove this discovery first. So we had no choice but to let him into the circle."

"Blackmail?" Trudy asked. "You, Marvin Irving, the Bouncer himself, are allowing yourself to be blackmailed?"

"If you're thinking I should do something to just make the problem go away, I'm not the Mafia," Irving said. "I don't do that. And even if I were the type, the person in question is connected."

The wheels in Trudy's head were turning. "A well-connected man. Capable of blackmailing Marvin Irving. Somehow related to religion..."

"In Uganda..." Gerta said. They looked at each other, both of them apparently coming to the same conclusion at the same time.

"No!" Trudy said. "Absolutely fucking not! No fucking way in Hell!"

"I agree," Gerta said. "If he's in, I'm out. I don't care about being a part of such a discovery. I will not have anything to do with... that thing."

"You both signed contracts already," Irving said. "If either of you back out, then I will have no choice but to sue you both for far more than either of you could possibly hope to be worth."

"You bastard," Trudy said. "I knew. I just knew it. I knew I shouldn't trust you."

"I wanted you, Ms. Hollis, because you're the best. And you, Mrs. Lyndholme, because you already have experience in this region, and I've been told that the two of you, uh, work well with each other. I need you both in on this, especially if our, well, let's call him our guest, tries to twist any findings we procure. I'm sorry to do this to you. I know how upset you both must be.

"No, you don't, you fucking bastard," Trudy said. "You don't have any clue, Mister Ultimate-Example-of-Straight-Masculinity."

"I'm sorry. I really am. But Harrison Bedford is going to be part of this expedition."

At the confirmation of his name, Gerta and Trudy exchanged nervous glances again. In America, there would have been some possibility that random lesbians would know that name. But here in Uganda, that name might as well have been a curse among the LGBTQ population. Or possibly the name of Satan himself, which was ironic considering he was a reverend.

In the United States, Reverend Harrison Bedford's home country, Bedford was considered part of the lunatic fringe. His "church" was classified as a hate group by the Southern Poverty Law Institute. Occasionally, he and his parishioners would make the news when they protested some Gay Pride event that the Westboro Baptists couldn't be bothered to show up for. It was only recently, with certain politicians in power, that his movement had started to gain any traction. Otherwise, he would be little more than a joke.

It wasn't until he had started to try his influence elsewhere in the world that he'd started to gain some modicum of power. In several countries in Africa, the Mid East, and Eastern Europe, his message that gays and lesbians were evil beings that tried to corrupt children actually found a larger audience. Uganda had been one of several countries that openly embraced his ideologies, to the point where he had been able to bend the ear of several major leaders. He had been one of several American religious leaders who had put money toward Uganda's infamous "Kill the Gays" bill, and the only reason it had failed was because some people attached to the United Nations had been web-savvy enough to cause a hubbub on Facebook and Twitter. That didn't mean that he no longer had power and influence in the region, though. Much of the continued criminalization of queer folks in the region was because of him.

And apparently, this man was going to be their new bestie for the next few weeks.

CHAPTER FIVE:
DRUNK ON BANANAS

The four of them weren't set to head out to Bwindi, where they would meet the three remaining members of their team, until the next day, so that left them with the afternoon and rest of the night in each other's company. While Irving had clearly hoped that this would be a chance to bond with his two researchers and had reserved them a table at the hotel's swanky restaurant, neither Trudy nor Gerta were inclined to speak to him at the moment. While he did seem to understand that Bedford's presence would put the two of them in a precarious situation, he didn't seem to quite understand the sense of betrayal that they both felt. As a black man trying to make his way in the predominately white business world, Marvin Irving knew what it meant to be treated like an outsider, to have to work three times as hard to go the same distance or make the same deal. He said as much as Trudy stormed out of the hotel room, and Trudy believed him. But there were different kinds of discrimination, different ways to be treated like you were less human than others. Trudy understood this not only as an African-American in academia, but also as a woman and a lesbian. She'd never been able to hide that she was black or female, but her queerness had been a secret to the world up until the mid-2000s, when she had finally admitted in a *Rolling Stone* article that she was in a relationship with microbiologist Barbara Nelson. For a while, she had believed things were getting better for queer people. People like Bedford had disabused that notion. Now, a little bit in American and a lot in other places in the world, Bedford's type looked like they were starting to win.

Actually, in a lot of ways, things were looking bad for people like her on multiple fronts. But specifically regarding this expedition, she was going to be stuck next to a man who had literally tried to kill people like her. Just because it was through legislation rather than with a knife or firearm didn't matter. For people like Irving, that was theoretical. For someone like Trudy, or Gerta, or even more so the actual gay and lesbian citizens of Uganda, it was a real danger of daily life.

Outside the hotel, Trudy was at a loss for a moment. She had known a number of places in Uganda and Rwanda very well once upon a time, but Kampala had not been one of them. There had been other cities closer to the Virungas, and in them she had known all the best places to get drunk. But beyond being in the wrong city, it had also been far too long since Trudy had done anything even slightly like fieldwork. Even if she were in one of her old haunts, the people and places she had known intimately would definitely be gone by now. In both countries, she had lost friends to AIDS, as well as the occasional violent political struggles. She had been in Rwanda for the Tutsi genocide. Some of the things she had seen then, well, she didn't want to remember them. There was a reason she had been a heavy drinker even before the mess with Killroy.

Wandering Kampala for a while, though, she found that her name still held a certain cache in this region, provided she accented it with a few well-placed bribes. After nearly half an hour of wandering among the crowds and traffic, she finally found the kind of place she had been looking for. Most of the tourists in her place might have sought out a bar, but Trudy had never liked those traps. The real spirit of leisurely life around here wouldn't even be found inside. She finally found her way down a shady and dirty alley, exactly the kind of place the typical *muzunga* would have avoided. At the end of the alley, though, she found herself in a sunlit courtyard. There were mismatched tables scattered around, all of them worn from spending years in the elements, as well as a large number of battered chairs: some folding chairs, some kitchen chairs, and even a pair of damp-smelling Laz-E-Boys. At this time of day, most of the tables and chairs were empty, but a couple of old men sat at one smoking hand-rolled cigarettes and playing cards. Off to the side there were several long boards held up by stools underneath. A tall, middle-aged woman stood on the other side of the boards, talking to a child that was playing next to a seventies-era green refrigerator.

"Hello? I haven't seen you around here before," the woman said in Luganda as Trudy approached.

"It has been quite some time since I have been in your country," Trudy replied, painfully aware of how out of practice she was in the language.

"You are a *muzunga*?" The woman looked thoroughly confused. It was a look Trudy had received often over the years and had learned to roll with. To a large number of the people in Uganda and Rwanda, especially in any place with some kind of tourism, there were two types of people: people who were from around here, and white people. The idea that someone from America or Europe might *not* be white didn't even occur to them. When people came to coo over the gorillas, they were white. When people came to tell them they weren't allowed to do what they were doing with their own land, they were white. And if someone was a scientific researcher, they not only had to be white, but a man. Even the word, *muzunga*, while not intended as a slur in any shape or form, included this assumption in the definition. They had literally never seen someone like Trudy before.

"Yes," Trudy simply said. This woman wasn't here to learn about the complexities of international sociology. She was here to help Trudy get drunk, and get paid for it. "Do you have Waragi?" she asked.

"I might. Do you have money?"

Trudy pulled out a handful of Ugandan shillings from a hidden pocket in her pants. "I do."

The woman beamed with a genuine smile. "Then we will get along very well." She pulled out a jar of murky liquid from the refrigerator, handing it to Trudy in exchange for a couple of bills. Trudy held the suspicious-looking fluid up to the light and appreciated its peculiar color. Let the tourists go to the official bars and drink the same imported swill they could get anywhere else. Waragi wouldn't be found in most of them. It was a moonshine made from fermented banana peels, and along with another moonshine made from pineapple, it was what the majority of the Ugandan population drank when they wanted to kill a few brain cells. And she meant that literally. She had, in fact, seen one or two people go blind from drinking it in dangerous enough quantities. This was not the kind of stuff that would ever pass an FDA inspection.

"Any chance you have one for me, too?" a familiar voice asked from behind Trudy. She turned to see Gerta coming through the alley. While Trudy's presence had barely been noticed by the old men playing cards, they immediately turned their heads at the sound of her heavily accented English. While Trudy might merit a spare glance here or there, Gerta was worth a full staring session. This was a *muzunga* as they truly understood them. It would probably be easy for a foreigner to want to characterize them as hostile to Gerta's presence, or wary, or even friendly, but Trudy wasn't going to simply assume how they felt just because they were locals and Gerta wasn't. Individual people were too complex for that shit.

Trudy turned back the woman behind the makeshift bar. "What's your name?"

"Nassuna."

"Nassuna, I'm Trudy. I'm going to need another one of these..." She held up the jar of Waragi. "...and a table where my friend here and I can..." She struggled to find the right word. "...have privacy."

Nassuna looked a little scandalized, but she also brought her voice down so the two old men wouldn't be able to hear. "How private do you wish it to be?"

It took Trudy a moment to realize what Nassuna was implying. "Oh. No. That is not what I meant. We simply wish to discuss some things without anyone else hearing."

Nassuna nodded, but again, given the look on her face, Trudy still didn't think she completely understood. She'd thought at first that Trudy and Gerta were looking for a place to get intimate. Now it seemed like she thought the two of them needed to talk about some other illegal activity. Although Trudy didn't like that, either, she supposed it was safer for Nassuna to think they might be involved in something that would be trouble for her if she talked about it.

Nassuna pointed them to a table under a makeshift awning. It was set far away from the others. Apparently, this wasn't the only time people came to Nassuna's meager establishment for something clandestine. Trudy gave Nassuna extra shillings to make sure she wouldn't develop loose lips, then led Gerta to the table and handed her a jar.

"Will this be the first time you've had Waragi?" Trudy asked her.

"I've had that pineapple stuff before, but never Waragi," Gerta said. "Anything I should know to prepare myself?"

"For the love of God, don't chug it. Nurse it, unless you want me to have to drag you back to the hotel."

Gerta opened the jar, sniffed it, and then took a sip. Waragi wasn't usually the type of liquor you were supposed to sip, but that was probably the best thing for someone trying it the first time. At her first taste, Gerta's eyes went wide and she sputtered, but after several seconds, she managed to swallow. "I was expecting the burn. I wasn't expecting it to be so sweet."

"So I'm assuming you followed me here?" Trudy asked. "Unless, of course, this place just happens to be more popular among the tourist set than I thought."

"Yes, I followed you, although you might be surprised to know I've been here before. Nassuna wasn't running it then, which is probably why she didn't recognize me. Her husband was. I heard that he died shortly after the last time I was here."

Trudy took a long, hard swig on her own jar, draining half of it at once. Gerta looked impressed. Also a little frightened. "What happened to not drinking it all at once?"

"I'm willing to bet my gut has a lot more practice at this than yours does."

"Would I be right in believing you've been giving it more practice sessions than normal, lately?"

"Is that why you followed me? To interrogate me about my personal habits?"

"No, I stormed out of the hotel for the same reason you did. I figured you were on your way to someplace where you could drink yourself stupid, and decided I wanted to do the same."

Trudy nodded, then took another drink. This one was a lot shallower. "Bedford," Trudy said simply.

Gerta nodded back. "Bedford."

"Christ, Gerta, I can't believe Irving did this to us. He might as well have invited a Jew to sit down and have tea with Hitler."

"Yes, well, sometimes people like Irving live in a bubble. They honestly don't think it possible for someone that horrible to exist, so when such a person is right in front of them, they cannot comprehend how bad it truly is."

"So what do you plan on doing about it?" Trudy asked.

"What can I do? Irving has us over a barrel. I know I certainly can't afford the lawsuit if I backed out. I don't suspect you could either. Also, there's the situation. Bedford or not, this is possibly big."

"Yeah, maybe literally."

"I want to be here for it. Whatever happens, whatever we see, I don't want to know about it by reading in *National Geographic*."

"You've been in *National Geographic*, though."

"Not as much as you, Trudy. But the point is that there will be history here. I want to be in the thick of it."

"Yeah, and maybe if we're lucky, Bedford will suffer an unfortunate accident while we're in the field."

"I wouldn't joke about that," Gerta said. "I may be in the closet, but you aren't. If Bedford happened to disappear or something under mysterious circumstances, his people would automatically blame you and come after you, whether you had anything to do with it or not."

"Well, then we're stuck with him, I guess."

"Still, I suppose we could always hope he picks up some disease and dies later. I don't think I'd be uncomfortable with that."

Trudy laughed, then drained her jar. Gerta wasn't even a quarter of the way through hers. "You going to drink that?" Trudy asked.

Gerta put a protective hand around her jar. "It may have already completely stripped my throat, but it's growing on me."

"Possibly literally."

"Yes, possibly."

Trudy supposed she could have gone to buy another, but for the moment, she didn't really want to leave Gerta's side. Given the magnitude of the enemy they were going to have to spend time with, Trudy wanted to be alone with a friendly face for as long as possible. Instead, she reached into yet another one of her hidden pockets at random and set the contents on the table in front of her. Grape jelly packets, this time. She ripped off the end of one packet and began to suck on it. Gerta grinned.

"I forgot about that particular habit."

"Yep. Still with me after all these years."

"I always wanted to know, how did your obsession with single-serving packs of condiments start?"

"Simple. I spent years out in the wild. Some at Bwindi, and a lot more at Karisoke. Eating the same bland food in the field gets to you after a while. Whenever I had to come back out for some meeting or other, I would always stock up on whatever was at hand, just in case I needed it."

"I always thought it was cute."

"I prefer eccentric, but from you, I guess I'll take cute."

An awkward silence fell between them for nearly a minute. Trudy made slurping sounds as she sucked on her jelly, and Gerta managed to reduce her jar by another quarter. Finally, Trudy figured it was time to address the elephant in the room.

"So. Married, huh?"

"Is it so surprising? You were married, too, in the meantime. And I'm sorry about…"

"Don't. Please."

"Okay. I won't."

"The difference between your marriage and mine is that I was married to a woman."

"Trudy, I tried to say earlier. I am married in name only."

"What's his name?"

"Arnold Vogel."

"So you kept your last name?"

"Arnold and I ended up compromising on a lot of things. We both decided that my name didn't have to be one of them."

"And the whole thing is a sham?"

"I am not attracted to men, Trudy. I always have been and always will be a lesbian. And Arnold is gay."

"So you married each other to fake being a happy, heterosexual couple to the world?"

"Yes. I will not get into what Arnold does for a living, but let's just say his profession tends to be conservative. He found it advantageous to pretend, and so did I."

"But this is the twenty-first century, Gerta. No one should have to hide like that anymore. Especially in Austria."

"First, do not pretend to know what it is like to be a gay woman in Austria. Second, are we in Austria right now?"

"No."

"No. We are not. I eventually got to a point where I had to make a decision. Pretend to be straight and continuing doing the conservation work I love, or come out publicly as a lesbian and be shunned in many of the countries I had to work in."

"But Gerta, that doesn't make sense. I'm here, right? I'm out of the closet."

"Really? Since you got off the plane, have you been walking around with a sign on your back that says 'I enjoy women'?"

"No, but give me some credit for being more vulgar than that. If I had a sign, it would say something like 'I like hot sloppy pussy.'"

Gerta waved a dismissive hand. "That is beside the point. You know that you would not dare hold hands or make lover eyes at me in public here."

"But that's not the same as faking a straight marriage. I mean…" Trudy paused. She still didn't want to talk about it, but it wasn't like Gerta didn't know. "I was married. To a woman."

"Yes. And you are also Trudy Hollis. You have a certain amount of privilege."

"Me? Privilege? I don't have any privilege. I'm a black, gay woman. Just what exactly do think my privilege is?"

"The privilege of fame and money. And of living in a country that is more progressive than some."

"Trust me, America is not always progressive. Especially not with all the political things going on right now."

"But it is still more progressive than some. In some ways, it is more than Austria, in some less. It is definitely more than Uganda. And even here, your notoriety gives you some protection. Once people know you are *the* Trudy Hollis, there are many people who will ignore that you are a lesbian, if for no other reason than they want their picture with you. No one wants their picture with me. And if I disappeared into a Ugandan prison, the number of people who would notice is significantly smaller."

Gerta's tone had been transitioning this whole time from her normal polite calmness to a deep anger raging beneath the surface, an anger that looked like it might be ready to blow at any second. Trudy was afraid she might raise her voice and make a scene, but instead, Gerta slammed what remained in her jar, looked cross-eyed for a second, and then composed herself.

"If I am dead in the morning, you will know why," Gerta said, shaking her jar at Trudy. Trudy herself barely felt a buzz, but Gerta looked halfway to drunk just after the one jar.

Trudy thought about something for a bit, decided it would be inappropriate to bring up, then decided she had just enough Waragi in her to justify an inappropriate question or two.

"Do you sleep with him?"

If Gerta was offended, she was tipsy enough that it didn't show. "We have just the one bed, as it would look strange otherwise. Sometimes, he sleeps on a cot when I am there, but both of us travel enough that it doesn't matter. Sometimes we do sleep in the same bed, but apparently, I snore."

Trudy remembered that. She also mumbled in her sleep sometimes, but it was in German, so Trudy had never been able to identify what she was saying. "That's not what I meant. I meant sex."

"We are married. Didn't you have sex with your spouse when you were married?"

"Yes, but apparently she had sex a lot more often than I did."

"Sorry."

"Don't be. I asked the dumb question first. But we were actually attracted to each other."

Gerta made a face Trudy couldn't quite identify. It was somewhere between embarrassment, disgust, and maybe even a little whimsical curiosity. "We tried once. Several weeks after we were married. It was interesting, but not satisfying for either of us. We haven't tried again. He is a sweet man. We get along very well. It's just that any love that may be between us is purely friendly. He has lovers on the side, as do I."

"You still should have told me before we slept together."

"You're right. I should have. I'm so very sorry."

"Maybe I forgive you then. I'll think about it."

"What about you?" Gerta asked. "Do you want to talk? I'm aware of some of what has been going on."

"Have you seen all the memes?"

"Some. I've seen the one with you and Killroy having tea together. I've never really thought it made sense."

"It's a meme. They rarely do, not when you think about it for more than a few seconds."

"I also heard a rumor that Killroy got a decent number of write-in votes during the last American election. Are Americans really that stupid and blasé about their civic duties?"

"Yes, they really are. But that was just a rumor. He actually got fewer votes than Mickey Mouse and Lucky Lady Duck combined."

"So what happened? If it's okay for me to ask."

"No, it's kind of not, but it's not like I could tell you anything that wasn't on the news."

"A little girl crawled over the fence and fell into Killroy's enclosure," Gerta said. "He made typical gorilla actions that some considered aggressive while others thought he was being protective of the child. Someone had to kill him to protect the girl. All of that, I know."

"Then why ask? That certainly seems to be enough information for everyone else to come to their own opinion."

"I'm trying to think of the words for people like that," Gerta said. "Uh, keyboard warriors? Might that be it?"

"Sure, that's a good enough way to describe them. They saw a headline of an article on the internet, an article they didn't even read, and they assume that's enough to make judgments."

"But I don't. I also know that you have not been seen in public much at all since then. That is unlike you. You did not even go on any shows to defend yourself, and that is something you always do. You will be a pundit on the news if someone illegally shoots a squirrel."

Trudy couldn't help but smile. "That squirrel is doing fine, by the way."

"Yes, I saw the cute videos on YouTube of him in his makeshift Lego wheelchair. That is not the point."

"Then what the hell is your point?"

"There is something you haven't told anyone, isn't there? Something in the story that never made the news. We may have only been intimate a couple of times in our lives, but I've paid attention to you since before I would have even be legally old enough to sleep with you. I see it. You are hiding something."

Trudy stared at her long and hard. Lots of people had given their opinions about her since Killroy's death. But not a single one of them had paid enough attention to her to realize this. Gerta was absolutely right. There something else in the story, something only she knew, something she had not told a single living soul. Such a little detail, but to Trudy, it changed everything. Now here Gerta was, confronting her, and yet doing it softly, gently. It would be so easy for Trudy to finally say what had really happened that day.

And yet, somehow, she still couldn't. Trudy couldn't let this go. It changed the very fabric of how she thought of herself as a human being. She didn't want to talk about it, and she didn't want closure. She wanted to stay mad at herself. She wanted to keep suffering.

"There's nothing, Gerta," Trudy said softly. She was pretty sure Gerta would easily be able to identify it as the lie it was, but she also didn't think Gerta would press the issue. "You know all the details. Killroy got aggressive. Knowing what I do about gorilla behavior, I made a split-second decision and shot him in order to save the girl. And that's all there is to it. Do you understand?"

Gerta nodded. "Yes. I think I do."

"Okay. Good. So then. What now?"

"What do you mean?"

"I mean, we can't stay here all day, can we? I don't think Nassuna would mind, as long as we kept drinking, but…"

Gerta waggled her eyebrows at Trudy. She probably thought it looked seductive, but she had lost just enough coordination to the liquor that it came off as slightly comical. "But there are so many other things we could do."

"Especially since we're not going to be able to so much as

touch each other as soon as Bedford is with us."

Suddenly, Gerta no longer looked so playful. "You're right. We won't. We've got the rest of today and tonight before we have to start pretending we are just friends. But honestly, I thought you would still be mad at me for not telling you about Arnold. You don't have to join me. Irving made sure we both have our own beds."

"Beds are overrated. I've spent too much time in the field to ever be totally comfortable in a bed."

"So what are you suggesting?"

"The hotel suite has plenty of walls. Floors, tables, couches, bathrooms…"

"Irving and Axton might not approve of us spilling out of the bedroom."

"Too fucking bad. Irving should have considered that before he screwed us over."

Gerta stood up from the table and only wobbled a little. "Well then. Lead the way. No, really, I'm not sure I could find my way back right now. If you're lucky, I won't puke all over you before we get there. Waragi. Never again."

Trudy joined her. "That's what I once said, too. You can see how well that went."

CHAPTER FIVE:
A COME-TO-JESUS MOMENT

True to their words, Trudy and Gerta spent the rest of the day and night doing everything they could to make sure Irving and Axton wouldn't be able to sleep from the noise. They were only partially successful. In the morning, Axton came to breakfast with thick bags under his eyes and a scowl reserved just for the two of them. Irving, on the other, looked rested and fresh.

"You two are nothing," Irving said simply. "You'd be surprised what I've had to listen to while bodyguarding."

"We probably wouldn't be that surprised," Trudy said.

"Yes, you would. I'll give you a hint. One particular night with Chris Mackerson involved two men, three woman, clown shoes, and a bike horn."

Irving had hired a driver that would take them to Kabale, where their gear and the rest of their team was supposedly already waiting for them, before they would continue on to Bwindi Impenetrable National Park. After making extra sure that both Irving and Axton understood exactly how important it was that Bedford not find out Gerta was a lesbian, the two of them took a seat at the back of the vehicle, where they talked about various unimportant aspects of their lives since they'd last seen each other, neither of them daring to get too deep. Occasionally, they would allow themselves a stray touch, sometimes gentle and sometimes urgent. Once they got out of the car, after all, they were going to have to act like they had never seen each other naked.

"Oh, don't want to forget," Gerta said as they were about halfway there. She reached into her personal pack, rooted around for several seconds, and then finally came out with a simple gold wedding band. "Who knows what kind of details that bastard might see?" She emphasized the words with a cold glare at Irving and Axton. Axton had to look away. Irving just continued on exactly as he had through the whole trip so far, staring directly ahead of him and humming softly to himself.

"There's no indent," Trudy said.

"What?" Gerta asked.

"On your finger. There's no indent where your wedding ring usually goes."

"That's because I rarely wear it. It's part of the mask I have to wear. I don't like to wear the mask if I don't have to."

Trudy stared at Gerta quietly. She could barely remember what it had been like to be in the closet. Even long before she had announced it publicly, her sexuality had been a sort of open secret. When people saw her walk off to somewhere private with a woman, especially her employees during various pieces of fieldwork, it had been known that anyone who wanted to keep their job would also have to keep their mouths shut. While her right to marry had been newer, her right to do what she had wanted with whom she wanted had been with her for longer. It got her thinking about what Gerta had said. Maybe she had indeed had a certain level of privilege there. The thing about privilege was that people who had it rarely saw it until someone else pointed it out to them. Trudy herself had long ago lost track of the people she'd had to tell had it better simply because they were straight, white, or male.

"If you no longer felt like you had to be married to Arnold, what would you do?" Trudy asked.

"I don't know. I've thought about that a lot. And yet I can't say. I suppose I would divorce him, but I would definitely not want him out of my life. He is my friend."

"What if you came back to America with me when this is all over?"

"I know that the border situation in your country is peculiar right now, so I don't know how easy that would even be. But Trudy, what would I be, your kept woman?"

"No! Gerta, that's not..."

"I care for you, Trudy. I always will." She dropped her voice lower, even though she hadn't been so concerned about what Axton and Irving heard last night. "And unless I were to end up in a monogamous relationship with another woman, I think I will always be willing to drop my pants when you are around. But I have my own life. It is not in America."

Trudy could understand that, but the words still disturbed her. It took her most of the rest of the ride to realize why: Gerta might have other things to get back to when they were done in Uganda, but Trudy would just have an empty apartment, no job, dwindling book royalties, and a growing collection of empty liquor bottles. It made Trudy desperately want a drink right now, but Irving had insisted that she not bring along any of the booze they had found in the mini-bar. Instead, Trudy pulled out a mustard packet, bit a hole in it, and sucked it like a baby sucking on a bottle.

Once they were out of the Kampala traffic, the car took a long winding road deeper into Uganda. Trudy was surprised, though, at how well-kept the road was. That certainly hadn't been the state of the country when she had last been here. Trudy explained how the growing eco-tourist trade had helped the country, resulting in large numbers of tourists taking this very route into the Bwindi Impenetrable Forest, spending hours getting deep into the jungle just so they could spend five minutes taking pictures of live gorillas in the wild. As exploitative as it might sound, Trudy approved. If that was the only way to get people to keep the gorillas safe, then so be it.

Still, the closer they got to their destination, the rougher the road became. It was obvious this far out that there had been attempts at public works projects. It was just as obvious that whoever was in charge of them was not very good when it came to civic planning. The occasional road would go from paved to broken, then dirt, then spontaneously back to paved as though someone had completely forgotten to take care of the patch in between. They went over a short bridge over a stream that was in desperate need of repair, and had Axton clenching his teeth for the few short seconds it took them to go over, yet later passed a beautifully done, well-maintained bridge that was on a path few people apparently ever took. Trudy had seen hints of these new attempts at infrastructure during past visits. It was obvious they had made progress, yet still had a lot to go.

Finally, the car stopped at the village of Kabale. Or, at least, what Trudy had remembered as the village of Kabale. She was reminded of exactly how long she had been in semi-retirement from the field when she saw that the sleepy little village she remembered was now a small city of nearly fifty thousand people. Like it had been for so many other things, the eco-tourism trade had been good to these people. There was a full hospital, a small municipal airport, and two university campuses, according to Gerta. It was far from the typical way the west viewed what they considered backwards nations like Uganda.

The car pulled up to what looked like a small, refurbished church. This, at least, Trudy remembered. She had no idea what it was called now or who operated it, but it was often used as a staging point for expeditions in Bwindi Impenetrable National Park. Although the basics of the building were the same, it was obvious that tourist money was now helping with its upkeep. As Trudy got out of the car, she felt an odd mixture of déjà vu and unreality. There was much she remembered here (and probably far more memories that were lost forever to the hazes of time and alcohol), and yet so much was different. If Uganda had developed this much, she wondered, how was it even possible for these people to still be capable of a mindset that gays should be killed just for being who they were?

Then she remembered some of the things going on in her own country, the up-tick in hate crimes, and especially the fact that the central architects of Uganda's worst attempts at homophobia were from America. Sometimes, the United States might seem more civilized. But sometimes, it seemed like it wanted to jump centuries back.

People were waiting for them in the old church, most of them local officials that had heard the famous Trudy Hollis would be returning to their beautiful park and wanted to make sure she felt welcome. While Gerta, the driver, and Axton took out the few supplies they had brought and carried them into the main building, Trudy and Irving were both subjected to a large number of people in fancy suits that wanted to take selfies with them. Selfies, for God's sake. Talk about a technology Trudy had never imagined just outside the most diverse forests in Africa back when she had started in the early eighties. While Trudy was the better known of the two around here, enough of the people knew about George Irving through *Sell Your Soul* that he had a little celebrity as well. Normally, this was a part of the process she dreaded. Yes, she was that famous gorilla researcher. Yes, she had hosted an uncountable number of nature shows, written sixteen books, and been a part of one of the most famous nature photographs of all time. Yes, she had known Dian Fossey and yes, she definitely had a few stories to tell. All of that was supposed to be tedious and only barely tolerated as an expense of being able to do pretty much anything with gorillas that she wanted.

But that was the way she had looked at it before. Before her semi-retirement to the Cooper Zoo. Before she had befriended a gorilla named Killroy. Before a little girl named Deborah Lucille had gotten away from her mom long enough to climb over the fence around Killroy's enclosure. Apparently, none of these people here knew that Trudy was the one who had pulled the trigger on one of only a handful of mature, mating-age mountain gorillas in captivity. Either that or they didn't care. Probably the latter. Gorillas, to these officials, were not people. They were commodities that brought in tourist dollars. Then again, it wasn't like Killroy had been a real person to all those people trolling her and threatening her on the internet back in the States. Killroy to them had just been a momentary distraction so they could forget about how shitty their own lives were.

Trudy pushed away these dark thoughts, smiled through the pictures, and then finally escaped into the old church. From the inside, she guessed that it probably dated from some time at the turn of the twentieth century, back when missionaries had been eager to save the souls of people they considered heathens. Ironic, then, that there was still exactly such a missionary standing in the middle of the floor, his pose obviously meant to draw attention to himself, and his face clearly expecting Trudy and Irving to be in awe of him.

Irving did nothing but go look for Axton. Trudy, on the other hand, had been saving something special for just this moment. She went up to Bedford.

"Trudy Hollis," Bedford said. "It's an honor to finally…"

Trudy cut him off with a loud, obnoxious fart. She may have

been in her sixties, but that didn't mean she always had to be mature.

Bedford trailed off. "Uh, yes, well, really, it's, uh…"

"Can it, you fucking bastard. Don't you dare try to pretend to be my buddy."

Bedford folded his hands in front of him and looked up to the ceiling, as though he were saying a silent prayer for her soul. In the flesh, Harrison Bedford was hardly an imposing sight. He had skin darker than either hers or Irving's, and a patchy beard that he probably thought made him look sophisticated. Instead, it only succeeded in making him look like he'd had an unfortunate facial encounter with a weed whacker. He was short enough that even Trudy had about a half inch on him. He was also wide, but his width was not from fat. Trudy had never seen much more than pictures of his face, so she'd been concerned that some soft Pharisee televangelist wouldn't be able to keep up with them during all this trip would require. The stout man was all muscle, though, and while he was nowhere near the physical specimen that Irving was, Trudy didn't doubt that, if they were somehow forced together in a wrestling ring, Bedford would give him a run for his money.

Bedford finished his otherwise silent prayer with a loud "Lord Jesus Amen!" By the look he gave them all after this, he obviously expected someone to ask what he was doing, to which he planned to give a spectacular hellfire-and-brimstone sermon, but most of the people just ignored him and went about their business. Trudy tried to do this as well, but Bedford grabbed her by the arm and stopped her.

"Just a second, Ms. Hollis. I would truly like to speak with you in private."

"We don't have time for this. We need to go over our final supply check, load up our rover to get us to the drop off point, and then do a final briefing to make sure everyone knows what their role in this is going to be."

"Your role here is exactly what I would wish to discuss. I would do this here, but there are certain things I will be bringing up that I'm sure you don't want others here knowing about."

Trudy stared at him, using every muscle in her body to resist punching this piece of shit in the face. Was this bastard about to try blackmailing her? Did he have some kind of dirt that he thought was going to get the evil homosexual booted from this team?

Suddenly, Trudy relaxed. Actually, she was pretty sure this was about to be a hell of a lot of fun. "Sure. Do you have somewhere in mind where you want to go?"

"There's an office right this way," he said, turning up the charm that got so many people watching from home to send him their life savings every Sunday morning. Trudy followed him, stopping only long enough to look in Gerta's direction and give her a reassuring nod. Gerta didn't look like she was reassured in the slightest, but she nodded back and went back to inventorying their supplies.

The office was in severe disuse, and for some reason looked like it was mostly used now to store crate upon crate of Little League baseball gloves. Actually, come to think of it, Trudy might have been around for when they were originally delivered. Some charity organization in the nineties had decided they wanted to introduce the youth of Uganda to baseball, either not realized or not caring that there were a hell of a lot more things charities needed to be donating to the Ugandans other than sports equipment. Trudy couldn't remember for sure if she'd been here for that, though, or if she had just heard about it through the grapevine. Probably the latter. It had the cloudy feeling of something she had been told while she was on a bender. The office did have a desk and a chair, though, and Bedford pulled out the single chair.

"Have a seat, Ms. Hollis."

Trudy raised an eyebrow. "Thank you, but no. I'll stand."

Bedford seemed taken aback by this. He had to be the kind of guy that wasn't used to others not doing exactly what he told them to do. "Please, I insist."

"No," Trudy said simply. Just because she'd spent many, many years inside a bottle didn't mean that she'd lost so many brain cells that she couldn't understand the psychology of what he was trying here. She would sit down, and she would be his captive audience. That extra half inch of height she had on him would be erased, and he would probably find some other small thing to stand on, like one of the pieces of building supplies littering the office, so that he would be able to imitate his normal spot from a megachurch stage. How many people did he run into where that petty trick actually worked? Obviously quite a few, if he was so surprised when it failed now.

"Now, Ms. Hollis, there's no need to be rude."

Something about the way he kept calling her Ms. Hollis really annoyed her. She almost wished her name was still Hollis-Nelson, so she could watch him squirm with the knowledge that, despite the best efforts of people like him, Trudy had still been married to a woman at one point.

"Who's being rude? I'm pretty sure I have the right to stand if I want. Unless you're implying that it's impolite for me to not do everything you say?"

"I believe we've gotten off on the wrong foot, Ms. Hollis—"

"Trudy. If we're going to be working together for the next couple of weeks, then you don't need to be so formal. Or at the very least, Dr. Hollis."

"Very well. *Doctor* Hollis." His tone very clearly told her that he didn't think anyone had the right to the title of doctor if they didn't practice medicine, but he would humor her in this situation because he was just that polite of a man. Trudy wished she was sick just so she could barf on him.

"And how would you like me to address you?" Trudy asked.

"You may call me Reverend Bedford. May we have a civil discussion for several minutes?"

"Are you aware of my reputation at all, Reverend?"

"Somewhat, yes."

"Then you should know very well that civil discussion is not something I can promise. But I suppose I can make an effort."

Trudy loved the complex play of emotions on his face. This was definitely not the way he had envisioned this conversation going, and he was unsure of how to gain his power back. Trudy certainly had no intention of letting him have it.

"Good," Bedford finally said. "I'll be respectful of your time and get right to the point, then. I need you to walk away from this expedition."

"No." She made no expression, and kept as little inflection in her voice as possible.

"Please, hear me out."

"I'm sure you know by now about everything that has been seen? Everything in Irving's pictures?" Trudy asked.

"Yes, I have, and I understand their implications completely. I just don't think that you do."

Trudy shook your head. "No, you don't understand. One of the gorillas in those pictures is Kramer."

"I… that name isn't familiar to me. Should it be?"

"If you want to claim that you know anything about me at all, then you should. I'm sure you at least know the famous photograph."

Bedford bristled at this. "Yes. Of course of I'm familiar with the picture of you making a mockery of one of God's most beautiful images."

Trudy had to pause. Yes, just like so many people before him, he compared the picture to the "Adam and God" detail from the Sistine Chapel. But the way Bedford mentioned it, it was almost like he believed the ceiling had been created by God himself rather than a Renaissance painter.

"Um, yes, well," Trudy said. "If you know the picture, then you probably know the whole story behind it. Or at least think you do. Everyone thinks they somehow know more about it than I do."

"Dr. Hollis, all of this is beside the point. I need you to understand—"

"Shut it. I'm talking now."

Rather than "shut it," Bedford's mouth dropped open in shock. What shocked him more, Trudy wondered? Was it that he was being told to stop talking by a gay person, or a woman? Or just anyone at all? He probably didn't remember the last time someone hadn't fallen in and done exactly what he said.

"That picture was taken after nearly a week of hiking. Back then, it wasn't like what we're going to see when we go into the Impenetrable Forest now. Back then, it wasn't just a name. To the average person, it really was more or less impenetrable. People had done it, of course, but the idea of idle tourists walking into it just to snap a few pictures of the wildlife? No one would think of it. Our trackers had found recent gorilla spoor, so we knew we were close, but we had no idea how close until a single blackback mountain gorilla came charging at us."

Bedford, despite his best efforts, had actually started to look interested. "Did you have weapons?"

"Of course we had weapons, but you're an idiot and an asshole if you think they were to shoot the gorillas. They were for the poachers. Poachers were far more likely to kill us for butting into their territory than a gorilla was. But an unhabituated gorilla is still going to be territorial. I was young at the time, but I had studied under the likes of people like Dian Fosse, so I had an idea what to do. With a couple-hundred-pound gorilla barreling toward us, snarling and beating its chest, I ordered every single person in the group to stop, take a knee, and put their head down."

"You didn't run?"

"If you run from a charging gorilla, it's just going to chase you. But if you show it respect, act in humility, acknowledge that it has the upper hand and that it's your superior in that moment... well, he just stopped. We all sat there, shaking on our knees, as the gorilla shuffled around and sniffed us, nudged us, even took a machete from one of the trackers. He didn't try to do anything with it, by the way. He simply looked it over for a while and then dropped it, like he'd gotten all the answers he possibly could from it. That's when I looked up. I couldn't help myself. I'd been up close with gorillas before, but never, ever this close. I did something I should have known better than to do, but I was young, curious, fearless. I reached up a hand in the hope that he would let me touch him. Very stupid, I know, and not just for me. Gorilla physiology is close enough to humans that our diseases can infect them easily, and they haven't had the years that we have to build up immunity. I could have given him something that would kill him in a matter of weeks. But, apparently, I didn't have anything that infectious. And I wasn't the only one with curiosity. I wasn't the only one who needed to know. He did, too. There was no attempt for either of us to mimic any famous image, Pastor. Just two creatures, fascinated and curious about each other, suddenly discovering that they weren't so different. The photographer took the picture before we could actually touch. It spooked the gorilla, and he ran off."

Bedford waited for several seconds, obviously thinking there had to be more to the story, before he spoke again. "While that is all truly interesting, I still don't understand its relevance to the situation now. So what if it's the same gorilla?"

"Kramer is supposed to be dead, Bedford. My knowledge of gorilla groups and habits was still fairly rudimentary at that time, but I later came to realize that Kramer was a lone gorilla that had been kicked out of the group he had grown up in, probably after he'd tried and failed to challenge the lead silverback for dominance. As we followed Kramer's trail, we found evidence of him crossing paths with a new group, and eventually, he lured away several of the females to form a brand new group of his own. We watched that group form from the ground up, you see, which was pretty unheard of at that time. That group became our group, or my group, if you ask certain people. Kappa Group, according to the official designation we gave it. I documented them all. I drew and kept track of their nose prints. And I'm the one who had to identify their bodies when the entire group was found slaughtered."

Trudy supposed she shouldn't be surprised when she didn't see the slightest hint of sympathy from Bedford at this detail. Gorillas were probably just animals to him, maybe not even up at the same level of dogs or cats. A scene of carnage, with headless adults and crushed baby gorillas, meant little to nothing to him.

"I'm assuming you believe it was poachers?" Bedford asked. "It couldn't have been that one of the gorillas simply went savage and killed the others?"

Trudy almost said that gorillas didn't kill each other, that only humans were fucked up enough to do that, but it wasn't true. Gorillas sometimes died in fights for dominance against each other, and, more horrifyingly, alpha gorillas had on occasion been known to slaughter baby gorillas from a different gorilla leader when the new alpha took over. But Trudy knew exactly what that looked like, and this hadn't been it.

"Gorillas don't take each other's heads for trophies, Bedford. That's a poacher trait. They sell them. It would be impossible for a small group of poachers to bring down the body of a full grown male gorilla by themselves, let alone the bodies of a whole group, so they just cut off the heads and sell those on the black market. Trust me. It was poachers."

"Then how can you claim that this Kramer is still alive in Irving's photos? You must be mistaken."

"I'm not. I know Kramer. That's him. I never found his body, but I had always figured he'd been mortally wounded and wandered off to die somewhere where we could never find him. But he's alive. He shouldn't be. We need to know how and why."

"All of that is very interesting, I'm sure, Dr. Hollis," Bedford said. It would have been difficult to cram any more condescension into his tone even if he used a hydraulic press. "But it is still tangential to the much more important facts at work here."

"Well then please, by all means, enlighten my poor puny brain."

"Don't be like that. I have nothing but... respect for you."

It took every ounce of Trudy's soul not to start taunting him with "Liar, liar, pants on fire." Then it took even more effort to keep from laughing. She managed to keep it to just a hint of grin. However much of it Bedford saw, he seemed to take it as a sign that he was starting to win her over.

"But this is so much bigger than any question you might have about how your specimen survived. This is about the stone circles these gorillas have been forming. I know you've seen them in the pictures. You have to know what they mean."

"I know what other people think they mean," Trudy said. "As for myself, I'm waiting to see what other evidence and clues we might find in the field before I come to any sort of hypothesis."

"Clues. Evidence. Hypothesis. All buzz words that people use when they refuse to admit they are incapable of faith."

"Really? And what does your faith say about this?"

"It's quite obvious, Dr. Hollis. We're in the end times."

This was hardly the first time Trudy had heard such an absurd assertion from someone of Bedford's ilk, but it wasn't the response she had been expecting here. "You'll have to lead me through your thought process here. I'm not quite sure how you went from a collection of rocks to Armageddon."

"Do you seriously not understand what those stone statues

they're carving are? The large one in the middle. That's God."

"Yeah, so again, that's one theory. But I'm still not following your train of thought."

"Frankly, I'm not terribly surprised, Dr. Hollis. It would take a Christian to truly understand."

"Um, you do know that I *am* a Christian, right?"

"I'm sorry?"

"I'm a Christian. I was raised Catholic. I may not exactly follow every single detail of Catholic rules, but I still avoid meat on Friday's during Lent. I have a Bible I read. I go to mass."

Bedford glared at her like she had grown another head, and it was speaking Esperanto. That could be because people like him often treated Catholics as though they weren't really Christians, but rather some evil heathen idol worshippers. Or it could be that he simply didn't believe her. She wasn't lying, although she was certainly embellishing and fibbing a bit. She did consider herself Catholic, but rarely went to mass anymore. She did avoid meat on Friday's during lent, but mostly because she tended to drink her dinner at the end of the week. And she did read her Bible. She didn't actually believe a large portion of it, especially everything in the beginning that contradicted known science, but she didn't think science had completely ruled out the existence of God yet, and she definitely considered herself a fan of Jesus. Especially the beatitudes, the golden rule, various parables, and that whole water into wine thing.

Okay, really, mostly she just liked the wine part.

All of that aside, she still called herself a Christian. And as lapsed as she sometimes might be, she was pretty sure she was still much closer to following the teachings of Jesus than someone like Bedford. Just because he carried a Bible around with him didn't mean he lived it.

"Ms. Hollis," Bedford said again. Not *doctor* this time. Trudy took that as a sign that all pretenses toward civility were about to go out the window. "You have no right to call yourself a Christian when you are perpetually living in sin."

"Plenty of Christian denominations beg to differ. My ex-wife and I even got married in a church, by an actual practicing pastor." Not that it hadn't been a nightmare trying to arrange everything.

There had been plenty of roadblocks, and lots of people even then trying to use their religious beliefs to block things. The ceremony had needed to be performed by a Unitarian minister rather than Trudy's preferred priest, and there were still lots of people that gave her bullshit for it all. But none of that was the point. She had, in fact, been married to a wonderful woman, to the best of her understanding at the time, and did it in the proper eyes of any God as she might understand him or her.

Of course, then her wife had cheated on her and been caught embezzling from their charitable organization, the lying bitch, but Bedford didn't need to know any of that.

"All of this is just an attempt to distract from the real issue, Ms. Hollis," Bedford said. She could see his anger simmering beneath the surface, ready to boil out into the kind of true fire-and-brimstone speech that got all his followers giving him their credit card numbers. "You are a symbol of the atheistic ideals that have infected our fallen world. You may claim to believe in God, but in your many books that have led good people astray, you have claimed to believe in evolution. You are caught in your lie. You cannot believe in both."

"Um, I'm pretty sure I can. Lots of people out there do."

Bedford acted like she hadn't even interrupted him. "You have tried to convince people that these gorillas are just like us, that they are connected to us, that we are not truly separated from them and they are not separate from us. And there has always been one hardcore piece of proof that you are wrong: we can recognize God's divine presence. Animals cannot."

Trudy had to stop and think about this, not because he made any good points, but because his logic was getting so ridiculous that she had trouble following any of it. "So… what you're saying is that you're here to prove that, what, these gorillas are actually *not* worshipping anything?"

"Either they are not worshipping anything and the whole thing is a hoax perpetrated by you or people like you, Ms. Hollis, or they *are* worshipping something and it is a false idol."

"I'm still confused. How would any of that prove we're in the end times?"

"If you truly claim you are a Christian, then read the Bible,

Ms. Hollis. The Book of Revelations! The signs of the end times! It's all there!"

"Revelation," Trudy said, trying not to smirk.

"Excuse me?"

"It's not called the Book of Revelations. It's the Book of Revelation, or more technically, the Revelation to John. But I'm sure you already knew that, being as how you've studied it and all."

"You cannot fool me with your meager Biblical knowledge. Even the Devil can quote scripture, remember."

"Yes, he can. And I'm pretty sure he's standing right in front of me."

"We are getting off track again," Bedford said.

"Have you noticed that you say that every time we get to a point in the conversation where you're cornered?" Trudy asked.

"I am not cornered. But it is all a distraction from the real reason I called you in here."

"Oh, please, let's finally get to the fucking point. Enlighten me."

"You are to leave this expedition. This trip needs to be the domain of God-fearing men."

Trudy raised an eyebrow. This was about to get good. "Let me guess. You have some kind of dirt on me, don't you? Something that will destroy my reputation, and if I don't leave, you will let it out into the public."

"If it has to come to that, then yes. It may be unseemly, but I will do what I must for my mission."

"Cool," Trudy said. "Go ahead and release it."

Bedford, who had looked like he was working himself into quite the passionate froth, suddenly stopped and stared at her.

"I'm sorry?"

"The information you have to blackmail me. Release it. Let the world know."

"This is no time to be glib, Ms. Hollis. What I know will destroy you."

Trudy laughed, a deep, from-the-gut guffaw. This, more than anything else, seemed to disturb Bedford to his core, and he physically took a step away from her.

"This is not a laughing matter."

"You don't have anything that's going to hurt my reputation, Bedford."

"If you only knew…"

"Then tell me. Tell me what it is."

"If you insist. But I have to warn you…"

"Actually, wait. Stop right there." Trudy finally took a seat in the chair. It no longer seemed like the inferior position in this situation as she leaned back and put her hands behind her head. "Don't tell me yet. I want to guess."

"You… you want to…"

"Was it the time I drunkenly puked in Idi Amin's soup in the kitchen when no one was watching, then let the staff serve it?"

The stare Bedford gave her was priceless. "That… that cannot actually be something that happened."

"It was an accident, I swear, but the fucker still deserved it. Or maybe it was the time I beat the ever-loving crap out of a poacher with his own rifle? I bet you it's that one. I always suspected there might be video evidence."

The look he gave her now suggested that this might have been exactly it, but Trudy didn't want to stop. She was having too much fun.

"No, no, no. I've got it. It's the time I seduced the First Lady, isn't it?"

"Wh… which First Lady?"

"Oh, wouldn't you like to know?" Okay, so that one was a complete lie, but Bedford looked like he was about to shit himself, so it was worth it. She had, in fact, drunkenly made a pass at Nancy Reagan once during a reception at the White House, or so she was told. She actually didn't remember what came of it, except that she woke up the next morning on the back lawn of the White House with Secret Service men surrounding her. "Do you get the point I'm trying to make here, Bedford?"

"No, I have to admit that I don't."

"Nothing you can tell anyone is going to hurt me. I have no secrets. I've already got a reputation as a problematic woman despite everything I've done in my field. Nothing at all that you could say would hurt me. Nothing."

"Not even if it was involving the unfortunate incident at the Cooper Memorial Zoo?"

For once, Trudy was truly glad that she hadn't had anything to drink recently. If she had, then she might not have been able to control her emotions. There was, in fact, that one last thing about Killroy's death that no one had reported. But it was impossible for anyone else to know it. She had not told a single soul, and there was no evidence anywhere of it on any of the security footage of the incident. She knew that, because she had reviewed the tapes thousands of times just to make sure.

"Nothing you could say about that day can wreck my reputation any more than it already has," Trudy said. She hoped that nothing in her inflection gave away that there was actually something for her to be worried about here. "And no insult you can throw out me can be worse than the things that have already said. You don't frighten me, Bedford. I've already been destroyed by the trolls of the internet. Anything you try to do after that is amateur hour."

"I wouldn't be so sure about that. What I have…"

"What you have either supports my earlier image as the brilliant but slightly psycho bad girl of science, or else it doesn't come close to destruction already done to my reputation from the Killroy incident. You made a very poor move here today, Bedford. You tried to take away something important from someone who has already lost everything. That's not just bad judgment. It's dangerous."

"Was that a threat?" *There.* Right there. Trudy saw something on his face. It flashed across his lips and then it was gone, but Trudy saw it, making the damage done. For just a moment, he had been honestly afraid of her. He'd given up any chance of holding a place of power over her. And even though he tried to cover it up, she could see that he knew as well that there was nothing else he could use in his gambit. This power play was over.

"I don't need to threaten you, Bedford," Trudy said. Which, of course, meant that her next impulse was to do exactly that, to point out that there were a lot of things that could go wrong in the Impenetrable Forest, no matter how tourist-friendly it might have become, and Trudy knew every single one of those things. If

Trudy really wanted to kill him, she could. Easily.

The memory of her final moments watching Killroy with that little girl came back to her. She had a very clear image of the last few seconds she had seen through the rifle's scope, the thing no one else had seen.

Yes, Trudy could kill Bedford easily. But she wouldn't.

She had to repeat that thought to herself again. *She wouldn't.*

If she had been drunk, Trudy would have stuck around for one final dig at the reverend, one more brutal mic drop that would really leave him reeling. When she was sober, however, and haunted by that day with Killroy, she couldn't bring herself to continue. Instead, she turned her back on Bedford and walked out of the room.

He didn't leave the room for several minutes. When he finally did, he went about his business prepping for the trip as if their conversation had never happened. Trudy supposed that meant that whatever secret he thought he had, it no longer seemed like the trump card it had first seemed.

Which was great, because the entire thing was a bluff. She was definitely sure she had done things while drunk that he could still use against her. But he didn't need to know that.

CHAPTER SIX:
"AND THIS IS WHERE DIAN FOSSE CALLED ME A WHORE"

Trudy met Big Isaiah and Medium Isaiah for the first time as she was doing one final check on their supplies. The two brothers introduced themselves to her in clipped English, said they were big fans, and then each gave her a bottle of booze: whiskey from Big and vodka from Medium. They said they had heard many stories about her and had been saving these bottles specifically for if they ever met her. She liked them immediately.

Gerta, of course, had to be the spoil-sport by pulling Trudy aside and confiscating the bottles when no one else was watching. "Trudy, you can't."

"I'm pretty sure you're not the boss of me, Gerta."

"That is the logic of a child. You are no child. You are a professional."

"Not according to most of the internet."

"Do you see any computers out here? Smartphones? Even traffic cameras that can accidentally pick up your image and later get hacked? No. The jungle may not be the dangerous and pristine wilderness it once was, but it hasn't come to that point yet. So stop wallowing in your misery and worrying what people will think about you. For the next week, maybe more, the only people whose opinion of you is going to matter is your six companions. And we won't think much of you if you drunkenly fall off a mountain and die."

Trudy stared at Gerta for a long time with a neutral expression. Gerta gave the exact same look right back. It was easy to forget how much time had passed since that long ago first naked encounter with this woman at the camp at Karisoke. Gerta had still been learning who she was and what she wanted to do in the world. Now, for the first time, Trudy saw the subtle lines of age and wisdom on her face. She may have aged incredibly well, but she had still aged, and with dignity. Trudy realized, for the first time, that it was a dignity that she herself did not share, and a rare shame came over her.

"Gerta," Trudy said quietly. "I don't think I can go that long without something. Maybe once, but not anymore. I won't be at my best."

"Trudy, do you trust me?"

"I guess."

"It's a yes or no question."

Trudy sighed. "Yes."

"Then believe me when I say this: you have not been your best for a very long time. And this has nothing to do with Killroy."

Trudy's initial reaction was to rage against Gerta and go storming off, maybe to even do something horrible like out the woman to Bedford out of pure spite. As soon as that thought came to her, though, she was horrified with herself.

"Go ahead and take that booze," Trudy said quietly. "Hide it somewhere if you want. But I want it back when the expedition is over. It was a gift. To me. From people who respect me."

"You say that as though you don't think anyone respects you anymore. You have to believe me when I say that they do. Or at the very least, I do."

Trudy turned away, waving Gerta off so she wouldn't see what Gerta did with the booze. This was going to be a very long trip if she had to do the entire thing sober, but she figured she owed it to Kramer. And even to Killroy, in a way.

Gerta came back several minutes later with a peace offering: ten packets of mayonnaise. Trudy was fully aware that it was odd for her to feel so touched by the gift.

Finally, they were all packed into two beat-up land rovers. The Isaiahs took the wheels, since they made the trip to the initial staging point quite often. Axton and Irving chose to ride in one together, and Bedford got in the other. There was a silent moment between Gerta and Trudy where they looked at both vehicles. Finally, Trudy gestured for Gerta to get in the rover with Irving and Axton while she went for the one with Bedford. Gerta nodded to her, a silent thank-you for throwing herself in front of this particular bullet. Trudy figured that the antagonism between herself and Bedford was already at its peak and couldn't get worse, while there was still the possibility of him finding out Gerta's secret and targeting her for harassment right alongside Trudy. Gerta, after all, wouldn't be able to hide behind the same shield of audacity that Trudy did. She honestly had something to lose.

Thankfully, Bedford wasn't interested in rehashing their conversation as they made the final ride to the expedition's staging point. He simply stared out the window for the whole ride, not even acknowledging Trudy's presence.

There were a couple of local volunteers at the staging point who helped them unload their gear and took possession of the vehicles. Once that was over, the seven adventurers stood on a tall hill, looking out over their destination. The Bwindi Impenetrable Forest. The northeast border of the Virunga volcano chain. And the only place in the entire world where mountain gorillas lived wild.

Trudy had to stop and take a long moment to enjoy the view. When was the last time she had been in the Virungas, anyway? She was ashamed to admit that she didn't remember, although she did know that she'd last approached them from Rwanda rather than Uganda. The blanket of foliage that spread out before them for uncountable miles all around held so many memories for her. The best years of her life had been spent here. Despite so many setbacks and hardships, she had been so happy here once. Every single thing she saw reminded her of a time that was lost to her.

"You see that tree over there?" Trudy asked, pointing at an especially tall tree that poked out slightly over the canopy of the rest.

"Yeah," Irving said. "Is there something special about it?"

"Very special," Trudy replied.

"Well, what is it?" Bedford asked. Oh, out of all the people in the group who could have asked her that question, it had to be him.

"That," Trudy said proudly, "is where Dian Fosse called me a whore."

Gerta snorted, and both Irving and Axton chuckled. Medium Isaiah smiled, but Big Isaiah just frowned until Medium translated the word *whore* into Swahili for him. Bedford was the only one out of all of them that didn't look amused, which suited Trudy just fine.

With the mood appropriately set for the beginning of their journey, Big and Medium led them down the hill and into the outer tree line. Gerta hung back, and gestured for Trudy to do the same. When she was sure the others were out of earshot, Gerta whispered, "Is that really where Dian Fosse called you a whore?"

"Don't be silly, Gerta. I was joking."

"Oh." Gerta actually looked disappointed.

"She did it in Rwanda, not Uganda. And the actual word she used in Swahili is so bad that it doesn't have a proper translation in English."

Thus satisfied, they both followed the others.

They weren't even fifteen minutes into the forest before it became evident that two of the members of their party had clearly not prepared for this. Irving, despite what Trudy would have thought of as a pampered lifestyle, had no problem. His intimidating physique was obviously not just for the cameras, and he kept pace easily. But both Bedford and Axton were huffing and wheezing with very little provocation, forcing them to take frequent breaks that Trudy would have much rather wanted to skip. This did, however, provide them with ample time to discuss their plan of action for this trip.

"It's a shame we weren't all able to meet at the hotel in Kampala first," Trudy said. "It would be easier to do this without the threat of rain or bird shit falling on our heads."

"Mr. Irving has told us little about what we are doing here," Medium Isaiah said. While both of the Isaiahs spoke English, he was the one who seemed to have a better handle on it, and his older brother allowed him to do most of the talking. "But it is regarding what happened to those two groups of poachers, yes?"

"Wait, two?" Trudy asked. She looked at Irving like he had been hiding something from her, but he shrugged.

"I only knew about the one group."

"The second attack was discovered two days ago. It is still being investigated by some, but officials are trying to keep it quiet," Medium said. "They are afraid it will scare off tourists."

"Oh God," Gerta said. "Please say it was not tourists this

time."

"No, I do not think they would have been able to hide it so well if rich white people had died. It was again poachers. This was much the same as the first time," Medium said. "They looked like the hand of God himself came down out of the sky and smeared them in the brush."

"Not God," Big said in a scolding tone to his brother. "The Devil. He is punishing the wicked. And we should not be interfering with his business."

Medium said something in Swahili that Trudy couldn't quite translate, a word or dialect that might have come about after she had last been here. Loosely translated, though, she believed it meant something along the line of *fucking dumbass*. "Do not talk like that. There is a *muzunga* here."

Gerta cocked her head. Trudy couldn't tell just from her look whether she was insulted or intrigued. "What does my presence have to do with it?"

"My brother thinks it reflects poorly on us when I discuss the things I know to be true," Big said.

"And by that, he means we look like superstitious idiots," Medium said. "*Muzungas* already like to look down on us for any reason. We don't want to give them those reasons so easily."

"My brother is…" Big struggled for a moment to find the word. "Uptight. It should not matter what any Westerners think of us."

Bedford finally spoke up. "You're right, my friend. I do in fact think this could be the Devil himself."

Big gleamed with approval. Everyone gave Bedford dirty looks. Bedford didn't take notice of any of it. He was about to get on a roll. "But you must be careful in saying that the Adversary can be allowed to wander the Earth. If he is in fact out there, we must destroy him. Mister…" It suddenly seemed to occur to Bedford that he couldn't call Big by his last name if he didn't actually know what it was. "I'm sorry, I didn't quite catch your name?"

"Isaiah."

"No, your full name."

"Big Isaiah."

"Um, yes. Well, Mister, uh, Big, you seem to me to be a perfectly God-fearing person. Would you care to pray with me that our mission is a success?"

Trudy rolled her eyes as the two men found a place to kneel and pray. While she waited for them to finish, she pulled out a couple of mustard packets. She offered one to both Irving and Axton. Irving politely declined. Axton, however, eyed the packet suspiciously before taking it and ripping it open to suck on it in much the same manner as Trudy.

"Make sure you hand the empty packet back to me when you're finished with it so I can properly get rid of it when we get back to the city," Trudy said. "And so help me, if I see you or anyone throw a packet or any other garbage into the forest, I will skin you alive. I'm not fucking kidding."

Axton's wide eyes told her that he completely believed she was capable of doing it. Trudy turned to Gerta to offer her a packet as well, then stopped when she saw that Gerta had found a place to lean up against a tree with her eyes closed and her hands folded in front of her. Gerta's lips moved silently in a prayer of her own while Trudy waited for her to finish. When she opened her eyes again, Trudy held up a mustard where she could see. Gerta waved it away. While Bedford and Big continued their own very loud and obnoxious prayer, Trudy moved closer to where she could whisper to Gerta without anyone else hearing.

"Were you actually praying along with them?" Trudy asked.

"Praying, yes. With them, hell no. I was actually hoping no one else would see. I don't believe in praying in public."

"I didn't know you were religious."

"Remember, there's a lot of things you don't know about me. We've shared a bed and we've been in the field together. We know each other very well at times. But we still have separate lives."

Was it Trudy's imagination, or did Gerta say that with regret? Did she really wish they could be more than just colleagues and occasional fuck-buddies? The idea appealed to Trudy, but it would never be able to work. Just because they were lesbians with similar interests didn't mean anything else about their lives were compatible.

When Bedford and Big finally finished, Trudy spoke up.

"Okay, so can we get back to the questions at hand? We can talk while we walk."

Medium gave a wide smile. "Yes! Like *The West Wing*! I know that show!"

"What's *The West Wing*?" Bedford asked.

"Never mind," Trudy said. "Not important right now."

This time, Medium took the lead, with Trudy immediately behind him while Big took up the rear position. Their slowest members, Axton and Bedford, were herded into the middle, allowing them to help set the pace.

"So are we going to a specific site?" Trudy asked.

"We will be going to the spot of the most recent attack," Medium said. "The bodies have been removed, but there has been very little investigation. No one much cares about a few dead poachers. We might still be able to find something of interest."

"What about the stones that were left around?" Trudy asked. "Will we be able to see any of them?"

"Gerta would be the best one to answer that," Irving said. "After all, she was the contact that originally photographed them."

"I was not entirely sure how to approach the situation when I first caught a gorilla building one with my camera," Gerta said. "So I took all the photos you saw and carefully marked their location, but I didn't want to disturb one yet. When I finally decided it might be worth the risk of removing one of the smaller stones for closer study, they were gone."

"And it was recent, too," Medium said. "Tracks in the area were fresh."

"Human or gorilla?" Trudy asked.

"Gorilla. Looked like several of them."

"You know I don't want to jump to conclusions without any evidence," Gerta said. "But it certainly looked to me like they maybe knew we were coming."

"You think they were trying to protect the stones?" Trudy asked.

"Maybe. It would fit the theory that they are objects of religious importance. But the evidence is thin."

"I want to visit one of those sites as well," Trudy said.

"Is that truly needed?" Bedford asked. "If there is nothing

there now, then it would be a waste of our time."

"Maybe," Trudy said. "Unless there's something specific about those particular sites that the gorillas find important."

"Do you think maybe the gorillas think those places are specific sacred locations?" Gerta asked.

"All of you keep jumping on this religious angle," Trudy scolded. "It's a hypothesis, but until we find actual, honest scientific evidence, we all need to stop assuming."

Out of the corner of her eye, Trudy saw Bedford raise his hands to the sky. "Bless the sinner, oh Lord, for she worships the false god of science."

"Shut it, Bedford," Trudy said. Thankfully, he did exactly that for the next hour.

CHAPTER SEVEN:
WHERE POACHERS FEAR TO TREAD

There was idle chatter over the next several hours between all the people in the expedition: the Isaiahs asking Irving and Axton about western culture, Axton and Irving asking about Eastern African culture, Bedford making the occasional attempt to preach that was usually shut down, Gerta talking about her husband and home in Austria in such a way that was obviously designed to throw Bedford off her scent, and, most amusingly, tales from Irving regarding his days as a bodyguard and early days of millionaire-hood. He had lots of tales of the musical artists and actors he had protected, always without the person's actual name to protect their identity. Not that most of them couldn't easily figure out who he was talking about.

Trudy listened to it all, but participated in none of it. Unknown to all of them, within her own head, she was experiencing her own roiling mass of conflicting emotions that bordered almost on the spiritual. First and foremost, there was the intense feeling that, for the first time in years, she had come home. It wasn't even until now that she understood she'd been homesick for the Virungas. If anyone had asked her two years ago where home was, she would have said her condo, in her bed next to her wife, or the Cooper Memorial Zoo. They were stable, lovely, prestigious. That was what people were supposed to want, especially when society deemed them too old to continue doing the fieldwork of their youth. All of that had been a lie, of course. The condo was just a soulless block of featureless rooms, her wife had already been cheating on her at that time, and the zoo... well, it hadn't been the zoo itself that felt like home at all. It had been her charges, the gorillas she cared for, and Killroy first and foremost among them. With all of that stripped away from her, she thought she'd had nothing but her liquor. Now she was here, back where she had truly started her life, and finally, she felt like she was where she belonged.

The liquor, unfortunately, was like a ghost that haunted her and kept her from completely enjoying the moment. She felt the need in her building with every hour that passed. She'd never used the term *alcoholic* to describe herself, but neither had she shied away from it. It was a part of her, a rather famous part of her, one of the legendary aspects of her identity. No matter how bad she got, she had always thought of herself as being able to function.

Now she was starting to wonder if she'd been deluding herself all this time. The urge to drink had started out as little more than an itch at the back of her mind, something she wished she could do every time Bedford piped up with some of his homophobic nonsense. But the sensation grew as the day went on. She wished she hadn't let Gerta talk her out of bringing the Isaiahs' gifts. She wouldn't have needed much, just a few sips. Gerta shouldn't have interfered, the bitch. If Trudy turned on Gerta when no one else was looking and decked her...

That horribly violent thought brought her out of her reverie, and she looked back at Gerta. No. She could never do that to Gerta. And the fact that the thought had occurred to her at all deeply disturbed her. Oh, she had definitely been known to stoop to violence on multiple occasions. But that was to people she considered her enemies.

Gerta was not her enemy. After all these years, she still couldn't come up with a proper word to describe what Gerta was to her, but it definitely wasn't an enemy. That thought went too far.

No, some deep part of her mind piped up. *There was one other person you wanted to hurt that wasn't your enemy. You know. You remember.*

"Shut up," she muttered to herself. Out of all the people in the group, she should have known exactly which one heard her, despite being closer to the back of their line. Gerta made her way up to Trudy's side. Trudy desperately wanted to hold the woman's hand, but Bedford was watching.

"Are you okay?" Gerta asked quietly.

"Fucking peachy."

"No you're not."

"Well, if you already knew the God-damned answer, why the fuck did you ask?"

"Trudy, look at me."

Trudy glance over, not wanting to hold Gerta's gaze for more than a few seconds. Whatever look Gerta might be giving her, whether it was pity, anger, worry, doubt, or anything else, Trudy didn't want to see it. Gerta, however, kept her expression neutral.

"You're going to be okay," Gerta said.

"Fuck you," Trudy muttered.

"You're going to be okay," Gerta said again in the exact same even tone of voice.

"Stop with the mind games, please."

"You're going to be okay."

Gerta finally stopped in her tracks and stared right at Gerta. Such kind eyes she had. Gerta had certainly seen her fill of terrible things in the world, yet somehow she hadn't let any of it harden it. That only made Trudy feel more inadequate.

"I think it's time for another break," Trudy said loud enough for everyone to hear.

"Not quite yet," Medium said. "The second poacher site is right up on that ridge." He gestured at a spot slightly higher up the mountain that they would reach in another ten or fifteen minutes. "We can stop there. And we can look around to see what we can see."

Trudy hadn't understood until now just how tired she was, and it wasn't just from the physical exertion or the effects of age. She increased her pace, eager to reach their first real stop, so she could stop and suck on some condiments in an attempt to quiet her raging mind.

When they reached the ridge, however, it became obvious that nothing about this place was going to calm her. Medium Isaiah had been right that the bodies had been removed, but it was still quite obvious to her trained eye that this had been the scene of intense violence. When she turned to look at the others, it was interesting to see which of them recognized all the signs of carnage and which saw nothing. The two Isaiahs, being the trackers that they were, obviously saw it, and probably saw a lot more signs of the attack than Trudy herself did. Gerta also had enough knowledge that she frowned and the matted down area. Bedford and Axton, unsurprisingly, both looked oblivious. Irving, however, had a slight frown, like he realized something was wrong here but couldn't identify exactly what.

"This is the place?" Irving asked.

"Yes," Medium said. He and his brother both cautiously walked along the ridge, occasionally bending down to inspect broken twigs and matted grass. No, not just matted. Crushed. Several trees were cleared away, broken at the roots and pushed to the side. All the underbrush in the area was broken, and in a couple of areas, large stones looked like they had been pushed down into the dirt. There were no signs of bodies or the poachers' belongings, but there were other clear signs that this had recently been a camp. Most notably, there was a small charred circle in the middle of it all that had been a campfire, but that, like everything else, looked crushed and broken.

"I guess I was expecting there to be blood still," Axton said.

"Anything that wouldn't have been cleared away with the bodies would have been food for scavengers within a day," Trudy said.

For once, Bedford dropped his holier-than-thou act and approached Trudy and Gerta. "Everyone looks very disturbed. What do you see here that someone like me doesn't?"

"Well, it looks like this entire area has been..." Trudy slowed down, not really sure if she wanted to say the word.

Gerta said it for her. "Stomped. It looks like a foot came down and stomped on them."

"No, that is not correct," Medium said from the other side of the ruined camp. Trudy immediately jogged over to him, and most of the others followed. Big continued his own inspections on the opposite side of the camp.

"Have you found something?" Trudy asked.

"I saw the photographs of the other scene, although I did not see it for myself," Medium said. "This is different."

"How so?" Gerta asked.

"It is bigger. It is also... I am having trouble with the word."

He said something in Swahili. Trudy thought she understood the basic gist, while Gerta gave an actual translation.

"Less defined," she said as Medium gave up trying to speak more technically in English and just said it all in his own language. "The other spot was a clear print. To his eye, it seemed to be a gorilla track, but far bigger than it had any right to be. This, however, is more like..." She cocked her head to the side, clearly puzzled by what he was saying. "An impact crater? Am I saying that right?" It was easy, sometimes, to forget that English wasn't her first language either. She said something rapidly back to him that Trudy was mostly able to follow. When Medium responded, Gerta went back to translating. "It's like something large fell out of the sky, broke everything beneath it, and then later just disappeared. He says this spot almost looks like... Wait, Medium Isaiah, that can't be right."

"Yes, I think it is," Medium once again said in English. "Look. I will show you."

"What?" Irving asked. "What did he say?" He turned to Trudy. "Did you understand any of that?"

"Some, but Gerta's right. There's no way in hell that can be correct."

"Are you going to keep us in suspense?" Bedford asked.

"If Irving or Axton had just said that, I would have told them right away," Trudy said to Bedford. "But just because it was you, I'm gonna go ahead and be a vindictive bitch by making you wait for the evidence."

"Sometimes I wonder how you came to be considered an expert in your field, Ms. Hollis," Bedford said.

"So does everyone else that's ever met her," Gerta said with a certain amount of fondness.

Gerta didn't seem to notice the look Bedford gave her, but Trudy did. *Tread carefully, Gerta*, Trudy thought. *Don't give him any clues.*

Medium brought them over to the edge of the ruined camp and pointed out a strange, wiry-looking piece of dark grass. When he picked it up, the piece was about as long as his hand. Now that she was closer, Trudy suddenly realized it wasn't grass at all.

"That's a strand of gorilla hair," Trudy said.

"It can't be," Gerta said. "I have never seen a hair that long. It has to be something else."

"I know you've been the one in the field most recently," Trudy said to her, "but I'm the one who's had access to captive gorillas next to an actual lab to study them and everything about them. And that's what a gorilla hair would look like through a magnifying glass."

"Over here!" Big called to them from the other end of the camp. "I have found something!"

They all rushed over to join him, but they could see his discovery easily without getting all that close. Big Isaiah was standing next to a large mound of gorilla shit.

"Oh wow," Bedford said. "That's one big, uh, collection excrement."

"Is that normal?" Irving asked. "Do gorillas just pick a spot and then the whole group uses it as their restroom?"

"No," Gerta said. "That not what gorillas do. They don't have a concept like we do that they need to have a special spot to relieve themselves. When they're traveling, they just go wherever they are."

"So there's no reason why they would suddenly change that habit now?" Axton asked.

"Nope. And this isn't the collective shit of multiple gorillas. See? It's not individual pieces. It's one, single piece of scat." And it was a single piece of shit that came up to Trudy's knees. Also, the color looked kind of different from what she was used to. "Gerta, could you reach into my pack to pull out a pair of gloves and a sample container? We better put the hair in a container as well. We're definitely going to need to thoroughly analyze all of them when we can get it back to a lab."

"This is just one piece," Irving said. "So does that confirm what I think it does?"

"More than you know," Trudy said. She waved her arms around to indicate the entire site. "Because here's the thing: the most common place for gorillas to void themselves is in their night nests."

"What's a night nest?" Bedford asked.

"Their beds, Bedford. When a group of gorillas settle down

for the night, they each create their own individual nest to sleep in. And unlike humans, they have no problem shitting where they sleep."

"That's vile!" Bedford said. "And you honestly believe these creatures are supposed to be genetically close to humans?"

"Don't act like humans are so different, Bedford," Trudy said. "In a manner of speaking, I've known plenty of humans too stupid not to shit where they eat. Gorillas shitting where they sleep actually seems like a step up to me."

Irving looked around at the remains of the poacher camp. It looked like he had caught on to what Trudy was trying to tell him. "And how big are these night nests for the typical gorilla?"

"Usually just big enough to surround the single gorilla."

"But this whole thing?" Gerta asked. "It can't just be one night nest."

"Sure it can, but it gets even stranger than that," Trudy said. "Don't you see? There's no tracks coming or going from the site. It's as though a single, humongous gorilla just dropped from the sky, squashed a bunch of poachers, slept and shat on them, and then flew off. We seem to be dealing with the single largest gorilla ever recorded, and either it has wings or it can jump incredible distances and with great precision."

"A giant gorilla with wings," Bedford said. "I think you may have been drinking again."

If Trudy had, in fact, been drinking, she wouldn't have minded that dig at all. But she could occasionally feel the physical shake of need for alcohol wracking her body. She was not in the mood for him.

Trudy went up to him and got directly in his face. For several seconds, he wouldn't move, but something about the way she held herself must have made him realize it would be safer to back up.

"That's the evidence we have, Bedford," Trudy said. "This is not a hoax. This is not the work of multiple gorillas trying to stage something. This is the thing that the large stones in those photos are supposed to represent. This is their god. This is the lord and savior of the mountain gorillas. And from the looks of what he did to those poachers, he's fucking pissed."

CHAPTER EIGHT:
RETURN TO THE GRAVEYARD OF THE APES

They camped for the night soon after that, although they all agreed that they wanted to find a site some distance from the ill-fated poacher camp. Big Isaiah kept complaining that they would be haunted by the poachers' ghosts in their nightmares. Medium Isaiah called him an idiot, which led to their conversation breaking down into light-hearted bickering in their native language. Bedford complained when he realized they didn't have enough tents for everyone to have their own, especially when he saw how close-quarters the tents would be. They had three, meaning three people would have to sleep in one while the other two held two each.

Trudy had been so busy fighting off her need for a drink all day that it hadn't occurred to her how much of an awkward situation this would be. Big and Medium Isaiah had simply assumed from the beginning that they would share one, and considering the size of them both, it was pretty obvious no one else would be sharing with them. And, of course, no one wanted to share with Bedford. Finally, Irving made the executive call that Bedford would sleep in the same tent as him and Axton, as uncomfortable as that would be.

The look Bedford shot Trudy when he realized who would be together in the final tent was priceless, but also decidedly disturbing. Either Trudy or Gerta would have been willing to sleep in the same tent as one of the men, but Bedford, apparently under the impression that he had some level of control over all this simply because he was blackmailing Irving, seemed to think such a thing would be indecent. Of course, knowing that Trudy was a lesbian, he also thought it indecent that she share a tent with the happily married woman, where Trudy might do wicked things to tempt Gerta away from a godly path. Gerta was the one who had to

90

convince him that her virtue would remain completely intact, but Trudy was sure that Bedford's suspicions about Gerta only increased.

As night fell, there was an attempt at a small fire, but a rain storm started up soon after and made any attempt at a hot dinner impossible. Under their soaked ponchos, the entire team discussed their plans for the next day. Trudy eventually convinced them that they next destination had to be the place where Gerta had first photographed the stones. Something about the photos was bothering her, and she wanted to explore as soon as possible.

After that, before turning in, there was some light chatter among them all. Again, Bedford wanted to say a prayer for their safety and eventual success, which Big Isaiah once again joined in. Gerta slipped away among the trees during this. Trudy silently followed her just long enough to make sure she was okay doing her own prayer where no one would see, then left the woman to her privacy.

There was one thing no one discussed, the elephant in the room that no one was prepared to deal with yet. Or, really, more like the multi-ton gorilla in the room.

As Trudy and Gerta slid under their thin blankets in their tent, however, Trudy could no longer contain herself. "This doesn't seem real."

"What, sleeping next to me?" Gerta asked, although she did it in a whisper so quiet Trudy had to actually ask her to repeat herself.

"I've done that before. That's definitely real. You know exactly what I mean. Why do you think no one wants to discuss it?"

"You could have brought it up, but you didn't," Gerta said. "So better to ask yourself that question. Why didn't *you* want to discuss it?"

"I don't know. Maybe because it seemed ridiculous. Like everything we found was just some hallucination I'm having from alcohol withdrawal, and if I mentioned it out loud, everyone would stare and me and tell me that I was nuts, that such a thing couldn't be possible."

"That's because such a thing shouldn't be possible," Gerta

said.

"And yet there it was. So what does it all mean?"

"Maybe we'll find out tomorrow. If we're right in assuming that in those stone formations, the large stone is supposed to be this King Kong..."

"Dear God, please don't call it that. The name might stick and we would get sued by some movie studio."

"If the large stone is the super-gorilla, then maybe there will be answers if we can find one of these normal gorillas building the formation again."

"Maybe," Trudy said. She had been facing Trudy as they both lay on the floor of the tent, but now she turned onto her back and stared up thoughtfully into the darkness. There must have been a small hole somewhere in the canvas, because Trudy could feel a slight trickle near her shoulder, but she had learned to sleep through much worse conditions in the past. Of course, she had done that with the aid of booze, so there was no telling how tonight would go. "There's still too many problems, though. Too many things that don't make sense from a scientific standpoint."

"Such as?" Gerta propped herself up on one elbow, allowing Trudy to see her face even while she was on her back. Gerta's pale skin was practically a beacon in the darkness. It was pretty, and yet kind of obnoxious at the same time.

"The biggest problem that I can see? Food." Trudy said. "You know as well as I do that the reason mountain gorillas are migratory is because there is too little nutrition in small areas for them to sustain themselves. If they don't keep moving, they'll starve to death."

"True enough."

"So they have to migrate a lot, because what little nutrition they get from grubs and scraggly plants is barely enough to take care of their massive bodies. So, logically, what do you think would happen there was a gorilla as big as the one we think is out there?"

It was Gerta's turn to look thoughtful. "It would have to migrate a lot more. Also, none of the food sources that typical mountain gorillas use would be able to keep it fed. Something that size is not going to be able to satisfy its hunger by stripping grubs from fallen wood or from little bits of wild celery."

"Exactly. So one of two things should happen. Either it should have just died from malnutrition already, or it would leave a path that we could follow. Broken pieces of trees it's eaten, or the carcasses of animals it's killed if it's been forced to go carnivorous."

"Which I don't think it has," Gerta said. "Otherwise, let's be honest, it probably would have eaten the poachers instead of just squashing them or ripping them apart. And it probably would have already gone on to tourists by now."

"Which I'm sure we would have heard of."

"I can think of a third thing that should have happened," Gerta said. "If it didn't die and it isn't leaving a trail of denuded forest in its wake, then in its search for food it probably would have wandered out of the Virungas. Someone would have seen it. As it is, farmers see normal mountain gorillas all the time when crops are grown close enough to the forests to encroach on the gorillas' territory."

"Good point," Trudy said. She went quiet for a while, thinking it over, before finally saying, "It has a steady and stable food source somewhere deeper within the Virunga Volcano Range. That's the only logical conclusion."

"But where? Trudy, this isn't the time of the early gorilla researchers like George Schaller and Dian Fosse anymore. The Impenetrable Forest in now, uh, I forget the word…"

"A misnomer?"

"Yes, I think that is it. The name no longer fits. The Impenetrable Forest is now quite penetrable. This is the twenty-first century. Everything is mapped and categorized. If there was something out there that can provide a food source for this type of creature, we would have to be aware of it by now."

"I don't know that I agree with that. It's kind of arrogant to assume the world doesn't have surprises in store for the hairless bipeds that think they run the whole thing. No matter how much we discover, there's always going to be still more out there we haven't made sense of yet."

Gerta giggled. It was a surprisingly young and girlish sound for someone her age, and Trudy couldn't help but prop herself up on her own elbow so she was again directly facing her. "What's so funny?" Trudy asked.

"You. You just sounded like Trudy Hollis."

"Uh, I *am* Trudy Hollis."

"Not just Trudy Hollis, but *the* Trudy Hollis. World-famous primatologist, defender of the environment, hero to millions."

Trudy snorted. "I don't think I've ever been anyone's hero."

"You have been. And you can be again. You just need to remember."

The way they faced each other, Trudy knew that Gerta was thinking the same thing she was, that this was the proper moment to move in for a kiss, maybe for that kiss to become something more. Trudy almost did it, too, before Gerta frowned and moved away. Just like that, the reality of the situation came back to her. They couldn't be themselves here. Gerta had to keep hiding. There was a man out there that thought he had all the answers, and one of those answers was that people like Trudy and Gerta were an abomination in the eyes of God. That not everybody thought of a supreme being in the same way as him didn't seem to bother him. His view was right, theirs was wrong, and while he might not be able to do much to harm the famous Trudy Hollis, there was plenty he could do against Gerta. Once they got back to the city, all he had to do was make one call to the Ugandan police and Gerta would be heading to jail for indecency and perversion.

"Maybe being in the same tent was a bad idea," Trudy said, once again very quiet just in case Bedford might be able to hear them.

"We are adults, not hormonal teenagers," Gerta said. She turned over and laid back down facing away from Trudy. "We can control ourselves." She said it with a distinct sadness and loneliness, though, and that loneliness haunted Trudy's dreams through the rest of the night.

In the morning, very few of their party were rested. The rain had continued all night and was still going strong now, and none of the people who were traditionally city folks had slept well in their damp tents. Irving was grumpy and moody, while Axton kept complaining that, with the amount of money he had allotted for the expedition, they should have gotten better tents. Bedford got the worst of it, as his sleeping spot had been directly below a sizeable hole in the canvas. Judging from the wry look on Irving's face when Bedford said this, Trudy guessed that this had probably been on purpose. The Isaiahs looked completely rested, though, and they even managed to get enough of a fire going that they could heat some dried meat and brew lukewarm coffee. Gerta had also slept well, which had been a source of frustration as Trudy had tossed and turned in the night. Her restlessness had been less to do with being cockblocked (and even after all these years, Trudy still had to regret that no suitable equivalent of the term had popped up for lesbians) and more to do with the crawling feeling in her stomach and skin. For hours, she tried to deny the reason for this. It was only as the first hints of sunlight began to creep in that she had to admit to herself that it was because of her lack of alcohol. She'd thought that it wouldn't be so hard to go without for such a relatively short time, yet the need was becoming all consuming. *Did she have a problem*, she wondered? It was kind of a stupid question, because she had known the answer for years, but it was only now that she was in a position where she had no choice but to confront it.

Today was another day, though, hopefully with a few answers to the mysteries before them, and Trudy did her best to concentrate fully on that.

A couple of ketchup packets helped.

When they were once again on their way, the Isaiahs had to change their route several times due to the persistent rain. Several low areas and gullies that they had planned to cross had been hit with flooding, creating sudden rapids that would be impossible for any of them to cross. Bedford grumbled at the increased walking, but Axton seemed to be adjusting. That was good, because Trudy was sure this was going to be far from the last unexpected turn in their trip.

"Where even are we at this point?" Bedford said after they had been moving for several hours.

"The Isaiahs are trying to find any gorilla trails, so we're going in a little bit of a roundabout way," Trudy said. "But we should almost be at the site where Kramer was photographed with the stones, which should put us right near the border between

Uganda and the Democratic Republic of the Congo."

"Irving, has everything been cleared if we need to cross into the DRC?" Gerta asked.

"Unfortunately not," Irving said. "I was able to make some deals to clear us through if we needed to head into Rwanda, but trying to get the papers to cross over into the Democratic Republic of the Congo was much harder. I tried to get us permission there, but there were far too many bribes I would have had to pay, and hints of instability here and there in the government that we probably should just avoid."

"The site was right near the border," Gerta said. "But if we want to investigate that big question mark we drew in the center of all the incidents, we're going to have to cross over."

"We should not do that," Medium said. "It might cause some problems for my brother."

"I am not welcome in the Congo," Big said. "There was an incident involving a stampede of buffalo."

"Well, we'll worry about all that if it comes up," Irving said.

Trudy only half-listened to the exchange. The closer they got to the next site, the more a sinking feeling came over her, and this time, it had nothing to do with alcohol withdrawal. They were indeed very close to the DRC border, in that area where they were no longer technically in Bwindi but not quite into the area reserved as other forests. They were, in fact, approaching territory she knew. And she knew it too well. There were decades of difference between what she saw now and her memories, but she knew these mountains, these ridges, these ravines. She understood now why the photos of Kramer had made her so uneasy.

"Hollis, are you okay?" Irving asked her. "You suddenly aren't looking so good."

"I know this place," she said quietly. There must have been something particularly grave in her tone, because despite her low volume, everyone stopped and stared at her.

"What is it?" Gerta asked.

"The site where you found the stones," Trudy said to Gerta. "I'm betting it was right over there, wasn't it?" She pointed through a gap in the trees to an area about a quarter mile up the slope from where they were now.

"That seems about right," Gerta said.

"Yes, that's where we were supposed to be going," Medium said. "How did you know this?"

"Oh God," Trudy whispered.

"I would appreciate it if you did not take the Lord's name in vain," Bedford said.

"Except I think it might be appropriate here," Trudy said. "I think everyone who was saying the stones were religious in nature was correct. But maybe not in the way you thought."

"Well?" Axton asked. "Are you going to enlighten us?"

"Let's get there first," Trudy said. "I don't want to be wrong and look like a fool."

The closer they got, the more a heavy feeling set into Trudy's stomach. It was probably just her, but she felt like the entire forest around her became somber and melancholy. The insects continued to buzz and the birds still chirped and cawed, the rain still drizzled and the air still had the thick, musty scent of equal parts growth and decay, yet all of it felt muted to her. It was like there was a screen over it all, and projected onto that screen were the memories of long ago, of her making this exact trek, of following other trackers who had discovered something, and who had immediately gone to tell her.

Trudy stopped in her tracks, only then realizing that she had taken the lead over everyone else. They stopped with her. Gerta came forward and tentatively put a hand on Trudy's shoulder. Trudy figured she should probably be worried that Bedford might read too much into the gesture, but right now, she could barely keep herself standing, let alone manage to care.

"Trudy, what is it?" Gerta asked. "Tell us."

"Gerta," Trudy said so quietly that only the other woman could hear her. "I have to have a drink."

"We don't have anything. I told you that—"

"Don't you fuck with me right now, Gerta. You're not stupid. I know you would have thought to bring something, just in case I got to a point where I couldn't function anymore. Whatever you have, give it to me."

"Trudy, you're being delusional. I don't have any—"

"Give it to me, you fucking bitch."

Gerta took a step away from her and almost tripped over something in the brush. "Trudy." That was all she said, as though just repeating her name would get her to come back to her senses.

And strangely, it did. Trudy became aware that everyone was staring at her, and several of them looked honestly afraid of her in that moment. What did she have to look like right now in order to inspire that kind of reaction? It was also clear that she hadn't been as quiet as she thought.

"I can't go any further," Trudy said.

"Just tell us what's wrong," Gerta said. "We can help."

"I can't, okay? I just can't. The rest of you go on. I have to wait here."

"No, Trudy..." Gerta looked back at the others, letting her gaze rest the longest on Bedford. She took a deep breath, seemed to come to a decision, then held out her hand palm up to Trudy.

Trudy stared at it blankly for several seconds before looking back up to Gerta's face. Her expression was soft, gentle, and yes, she was afraid of the consequences, but she also looked like she was ready to accept them.

Under any other circumstances, Trudy probably wouldn't have taken her hand. There would be no hiding Gerta's secret from Bedford after this. Yet she desperately needed that contact. She didn't know if she would consider what Gerta offered her to be love, but it was definitely comfort.

Trudy put her hand in Gerta's. Gerta brought Trudy's hand up to her mouth and gently kissed it. "We'll go together, yes?"

Trudy took a deep breath before nodding. "Yes. Let's go."

They continued to hold hands the rest of the way to the site. Trudy didn't look back to see Bedford's reaction, but she was sure it was the kind that could melt whole boulders. With Gerta by her side, Trudy finally started talking. Not a single other person in the group made a peep, every one of them listening intently to her every word.

"They woke me up just before dawn. Our base camp was in the other direction of where we just came, or else maybe I would have recognized the area sooner. There were two trackers, one who was very young and just training, so I didn't really know his name. The other one had a name that none of the other non-

Ugandans in the group could pronounce, so they just called him Mickey. I always thought that was disrespectful, but he actually loved it. He kept saying, 'Like the mouse! I love the mouse!'"

Bedford started to say something, but Irving cut him off with a curt *Shhhh*. The brief interruption didn't faze Trudy.

"Mickey and his friend came back to the camp early, but I was still asleep. I woke when I heard them shouting, and immediately, I was out of my tent with a machete in my hand. That kind of shouting never came from an exciting find of some sort. That kind always meant something had gone very wrong."

Trudy stopped at one particular tree. She put her hand on the truck and looked up, slowly caressing the bark. "Right here. This is where I stopped to lean after running all the way here. Mickey had been tracking the group all night because he thought something was wrong. He didn't really have evidence, he said, just a feeling. And when I stopped here, that's when I saw it all."

There was nothing about this particular patch of the jungle that should have been remarkable. That was a big part of why Trudy hadn't recognized it right away in the photos of Kramer with the stones. Just trees and bushes and a rock here or there. She wouldn't have remembered any of it at all if the scene hadn't been scarred into her mind. There were over two decades of new growth here now, and the trees were taller, and at least two were missing, as far as she could see. That smaller one on the far right of her vision might not have been here at all back then. Yet she still knew this place. It was like she could feel ghosts haunting it.

"Most people don't get it," Trudy said. "To them, gorillas are animals. But when you spend enough time with them, you start to see. Each one has its own personality, its ticks and foibles. Hell, even their own sense of humor. I've seen gorillas play pranks on each other in the wild. They may not be as sophisticated as wrapping a toilet seat in plastic wrap, but the jokes are there. Do you get it? They may not be humans, yet somehow they are still people.

"I'd lived near and with Group Kappa for nearly two years. I knew them. I gave them all names. There were two adult males, Kramer and Dutch. I could see the power struggle growing there, but Dutch just didn't have it in him to usurp Kramer's power. He would have relented eventually, or else he would have gone out on his own in an attempt to start his own group. There were three females, or at least I think they were all females. It's actually very difficult to tell before they reach full maturity. Rose and Crunchy were definitely females, as I had seen them have children. I actually witnessed it, in Crunchy's case, but her baby died soon after it was born. Then there was Turtle. She would crawl all over all the adults, getting into everything. Dutch seemed annoyed by her, but there was real, honest fondness in the way Kramer would play with her. He played with his daughter. As in something some fucking human fathers can't even be bothered to do."

Trudy stepped away from the tree. By now, they could all see the objects nestled in the center of the site, yet Trudy acted like they weren't there, like they weren't the very things they had traveled halfway around the world to find. Instead, she found a rock nearby. It was wet and clean in the rain, but in Trudy's mind, it was still smeared with copious amounts of blood.

"I think this one was Crunchy. Without her head, obviously I couldn't identify her by her nose print. Her wound looked like it was the quickest and cleanest, like the blade they'd used on her was freshly sharpened. After that, the machete or whatever they used must have been dulled by cutting through her, because none of the others looked like they had died quick."

She took two long strides to the north, where she stopped and looked down at a barely noticeable depression by her feet. "This was Turtle. Her death was probably the most shocking and senseless of all. Usually, poachers back then would take the baby gorilla they found with them and try to sell them to some less-than-ethical zoo or collector. Maybe they did try to take Turtle and she fought back. Or maybe they just had fun hacking her tiny body to bits."

Trudy pointed to a spot about fifty feet away. "We found Dutch over there. Him we could identify for sure, because the silver coloring was just beginning to come into the saddle of his back. It marked him as male, but younger than Kramer. Head gone, of course. His hands were broken, too. It looked like maybe the poachers had taken pliers to them. That made me think that maybe this wasn't just an attempt to get gorilla heads for the black market. The poachers intentionally tortured the poor creatures, and the only reason I could think that they might do that is if they were trying to get revenge on me specifically for something I'd done to hinder them. To this day, I don't have proof, but I still think that might be true."

"Rose we found further down the slope. It looked like she'd actually tried to run away, because there were a large number of bullet holes in her back. She was as headless as all the other adults, but looking at her, I couldn't help but think that she was the luckiest one. She was the only one I could be sure was dead by the time they started chopping her apart."

Now Trudy finally turned to the center of the site. As if this was an unspoken signal, everyone else in the party came to join her, where they all circled the six stones that had been placed in the center of it all. There was no denying now that someone had made a deliberate, if clumsy, attempt to sculpt them into the shape of gorillas. They were ill-proportioned and lacked any definite features, but the bodies, arms, legs, and heads were clearly intended to be there. Five smaller gorilla shapes in a circle (and one of which seemed even smaller than the others), each of them facing a much larger stone in the center. The center stone somehow managed to seem angrier in its rough cut, like it would go on a rampage if only it could be turned into flesh and blood.

"We were wrong this whole time, and yet we were also right," Trudy said. Her voice was still quiet, but now, instead of being caused by sadness, she could barely speak from awe. "The stones are created as art. And they are religious in significance. But we still didn't get their true purpose.

"Guys, these are memorials, or grave markers, or something similar. Kramer is mourning his dead family."

CHAPTER NINE:
GORILLA WARFARE

For the next hour, the site (or the graveyard, as Trudy couldn't help but calling it) was abuzz with activity. Gerta had her camera and carefully photographed everything she possibly could, right down to the rough sculpting marks in the stones just in case that could give them more insight into their creation. The Isaiahs put their tracking skills to use, searching the area to see if there was any sign that Kramer or some other gorilla had been here recently. Irving and Axton had found an out of the way rock where they spread out the map and previous pictures, the two of them talking quietly but animatedly about what all this meant and what they were going to do next. Only two of the party sat during this whole time. Trudy and Bedford both took seats on opposite sides of the carved stones and stared long and hard at them. Trudy had a look of amazement the whole time, while Bedford glared on with suspicion. Trudy could almost believe that he expected them to start bleeding the blood of Satan at any moment, finally proving all his suspicions.

"You look awfully happy about all this," Bedford said to her. He glowered at Gerta as she nearly tripped over Trudy in an effort to get a better angle on the center stone. She probably could have done it easier if she got in close and moved some of the smaller stones out of her way. However, not a single person had made an effort to touch the stones yet.

"I don't think happy is the right word," Trudy said. "More like I'm trying to process it."

"I don't understand what there is to process," Bedford said. "This is true idol worship. Everything I was afraid it would be."

"Come off it already, Bedford," Gerta said from behind the lens of her camera. "Even you have to admit what an amazing discovery all this is. Gorillas not just mourning their dead, but memorializing them decades after the fact. Only humans are supposed to do that."

Trudy nodded, but there was still more to it than Gerta seemed to realize. Once again, just like so much in biology and even sociology, it all came back down to food sources. A major hypothesis regarding how humans had risen to be the dominant species on the planet was that they had simply been in the right places at the right time, with abundant food and resources allowing humans to use their highly developed brains to concentrate on something other than simple survival. Humans had simply found themselves in areas with extra animals and extra produce, allowing them to develop animal husbandry and agriculture with the things they didn't have to immediately eat. This had then let to language, culture, art, and technology.

There was plenty of evidence of animals in nature with brains that could theoretically compete with humans, such as dolphins, whales, the occasional bird, and yes, gorillas. Unlike the others, gorillas had appendages that allowed them greater manipulation of their environment. So if they had the resources presented to them, there was no reason art and culture couldn't grow in their small societies.

Here was the evidence of culture and leisure time. They had developed tools of their own, and created art. So where the hell were the resources?

"Ms. Hollis? I was talking to you."

"Don't bother, Bedford. I know that look. She has science face. She's working a problem."

Trudy stood up and absently circled in place until she saw the Isaiahs quietly conferring with each other. She stalked over to them, now ignoring every attempt by the others to get her attention.

"Tell me what you see," Trudy said to them.

"There were at least two gorillas here recently, maybe about two hours ago," Medium said.

"Two," Trudy said thoughtfully. Odd, but perhaps not in the way she had originally thought. She'd almost been assuming that Kramer had set up these stones all alone, but even for a gorilla it would be difficult to carry them. And it also made sense, now that Trudy thought of it, since it would be highly unlikely for Kramer to live all by himself for so long. If he survived the original attack, then eventually he would have sought out another group to join. Gorillas were nothing if not social creatures.

Which was the real reason why two gorillas was a strange number: there should have been more.

"Find any scat?" Trudy asked.

"Some over there," Big said. "It looked strange, though."

"Strange how?" Trudy asked, although she suspected she already knew the answer.

"It is a different thickness and color than usual," Medium said.

Trudy nodded. "And have you found any evidence that the two gorillas ate anything in this area?"

Medium looked surprised. "No. Now that you say it, I do not think I have seen any."

"Show me the gorilla bolus you found," Trudy said as she pulled off her pack and dug around inside for a pair of gloves. Once she had them on, she went over to the gorilla shit, gave it a cursory inspection, and then took it right over to Irving and Axton. Never one to miss a dramatic moment, Trudy dropped the turd directly in the center of their map.

"Dude!" Axton said, scrambling away from the brown mountain that suddenly sprung up in front of him.

"Did you seriously just say 'dude'?" Trudy asked him.

"Hollis, what the hell are you doing?" Irving asked.

"Everyone gather around. You need to see this."

The others formed a circle around the map sitting on the rock. Bedford's face somehow became even more disdainful when he saw what was now in the center of it. "Ms. Hollis, honestly. Just when I thought you couldn't get any more crude."

"Look at it," Trudy said. "Truly look at it."

Neither Axton or Bedford took her up on her offer, but Irving, Gerta, and the Isaiahs bent in for a closer look.

"Does anyone else see it?" Trudy asked.

"It looks just like a normal piece of shit to me," Irving said.

"That's because you're used to looking at human shit."

"Hand me a glove," Gerta said to her. Trudy handed her one,

and once she had it on, Gerta gave a few pokes to look deeper into the bolus. She didn't have to go far to see the things that shouldn't be there. "Corn," Gerta said.

"And some other grains," Trudy said with a nod.

"So?" Axton asked. "I was under the impression that it wasn't unheard of for gorillas to invade local farms that were too close to the forest."

"You're right. That does happen," Trudy said. "Except most of those grains you see half-digested in there are not supposed to be grown in this region. And not just that, but there are things that should be in there but aren't. No evidence of wild celery or grubs or any of the typical plants we should be seeing in a gorilla's diet. So does anyone want to ask the hundred thousand dollar question?"

"I guess I will," Irving said. "Where are they getting food that shouldn't grow around here?"

"Right," Trudy said. She unceremoniously picked up the scat and tossed it aside, then pointed at the brown stain it had left on the map right over the large question mark. "We've got to go deeper into the mountains. That's where we'll find our answer."

"Answer to what?" Bedford asked.

"The answer to all of this. Where and what the gorillas are eating, how a small number of gorillas can spontaneously develop arts and culture, and probably most importantly, if there is a giant gorilla out there squashing people and how it can exist in the first place."

"Why are you so hung up on the thing about art?" Bedford asked. "I thought I'd heard of that before. Something about a gorilla that painted. I thought they called it..."

Gerta, Irving, and Axton all said it at the same time. "Don't mention Koko."

"No, wait, go right ahead," Trudy said.

"Really?" Gerta asked.

"Koko has her own basic understanding of language and arts because she was socialized into it by the humans around her. So if it could happen to her, why not to others?"

"You think someone taught them to sculpt?" Gerta asked.

"Maybe. Or maybe they found something that pushed them

along to the next level. Either way, whatever it is, it's somewhere deeper in the Virungas."

After that, there wasn't much else to do but pack up and prepare to push deeper in the jungle and mountains. There was, however, one more argument that needed to be had.

"No. Absolutely not," Trudy said.

"Hollis, I'm surprised at you," Irving said. He and Bedford were standing on side of the circle of stones while Trudy and Gerta stood on the other. Irving had his own gloves on along with a sample bag in hand, but Trudy had stopped him before he could grab the smallest of the carved stones and store it away.

"It's disrespectful," Trudy said.

"They're animals, Dr. Hollis," Bedford said. "You can't be disrespectful to an animal. I believe you keep forgetting that they're not human."

"Seriously?" Trudy asked him. "I don't understand you. Have you forgotten the fucking color of our skin? Have you forgotten that in the not-too-distant history of our species white people said those exact words about people like us? Still say them, in fact, among certain groups."

"The two things are nothing alike," Bedford said.

"Of course you would say that," Trudy said. "You've made your entire career out of saying that about people that were different. Except instead of skin color or species, you like to focus on who people love."

"What people like you..." Bedford gestured at both Trudy and Gerta, making it perfectly clear that Gerta's secret was thoroughly blown at this point. "...do with each other is a choice, specifically a choice to turn your back on the destiny that God gave you." He looked specifically at Gerta. "Does your husband know you're a pervert?"

Trudy tensed, not sure at all what Gerta would do. She was surprised when the woman actually smiled. "He's quite fond of it, actually, as long as he gets to watch once in a while."

Even though Trudy knew damned well he did nothing of the sort, she still thoroughly enjoyed the look of abject horror on Bedford's face.

"All of that is off track," Irving said. "We came all the way out here to find evidence of exactly this sort of thing." He gestured at the stones. "We can't just walk away without taking one to study."

"I have to agree with Trudy," Gerta said. "If she is truly right, then taking one would be similar to desecrating a grave. In case you forget, they previously moved the stones when they thought we might find them. Keeping them safe has to be important to them."

"If we go back without one, no one will believe what we've discovered," Irving said.

"Bullshit," Trudy said. "Gerta took tons of pictures. We have more than enough evidence."

"But there are things we wouldn't be able to learn from just the pictures," Irving said. "Like what kind of stone they used. Or the sculpting marks can be studied to learn more about the types of tools they use. Anything we learn can not only help us understand, but also help us help the gorillas. When this is finally revealed, we can get this whole area turned into a sanctuary. They can be left in peace. But all of that depends on people believing us."

"And our word wouldn't be enough?" Trudy asked.

Irving paused. Trudy, unfortunately, knew exactly what he was going to say before it was even out of his mouth. "We both know I trust you, Hollis. You wouldn't be here if I didn't. But the rest of the world doesn't anymore."

"But taking one of the stones, it would be like..." She trailed off. Gerta had already said it best, that doing so would be like desecrating a grave, but in order for that argument to hold any water, first Bedford and Irving would have to acknowledge that these gorillas hadn't just been animals. When Trudy had seen their slaughtered bodies, it had been like she walked into her own living room and found that someone had broken in and murdered her entire family.

But Irving was the one funding the expedition. If he said they were taking one of the stones back with them, Trudy ultimately couldn't stop him. If she tried, he could always send her back and keep her from being a part of everything else that still needed to be discovered.

Gerta silently took Trudy's hand. Bedford, seeing this,

stormed off in disgust. Irving, on the other hand, took this as evidence that they weren't going to stop him. He carefully wrapped the smallest stone, the one Trudy was sure was supposed to represent Turtle, and stashed it gently at the bottom of his pack.

"If we're all ready, let's move," Irving said. "There's a lot of ground to cover, and since we're not even completely sure what we're looking for…"

"We know enough," Gerta said. "Look for large sources of food that shouldn't be there. More evidence of tools."

"And don't forget the giant fucking footprints," Trudy said.

"This way," Big Isaiah said. "We will follow the trail the gorillas left for us. Eventually, they need to go back to their food, yes?"

Despite losing the argument with Irving, Trudy still found herself buoyed by their discovery. The intense urge for alcohol still followed her, but the thrill of discovering something new for the first time in years gave her enough of a boost that she was able to ignore the need for now. She was even feeling a little frisky, now that she didn't have to hide her attraction to Gerta, but just because that particular secret was now in the open, that didn't mean the rest of the party would be amenable to Gerta and Trudy finding a place under some deadfall and getting Sapphic. She did, at least, feel comfortable poking Bedford a little about it all.

"So, fine, you know by now that Gerta and I know each other biblically," Trudy said to him. Gerta glared at her, a clear sign that she wanted Trudy to stop, but if Trudy couldn't drink, she needed to do something else to occupy herself. Usually, that meant acting like an asshole. "You planning on calling the cops on us as soon as we get back to the city?"

"It wouldn't do much good, now would it?" Bedford said. "You yourself made it quite plain that you think you are above all laws, both God's and man-made. As for her…" He gestured dismissively in Gerta's direction. "…we both know why she won't be taken in or arrested, no matter how much she sins with you."

"Wait, what do you mean?" Gerta said.

Trudy thought about it for a second. She hadn't considered it before, but now that Bedford brought it up, it was painfully obvious. "He means because you're white," Trudy said. "And a foreigner. If you were either alone, then maybe the local authorities might dare, but the fact that you're both means that you'll get treated like you're above the law. It would cause too much of an international incident."

"That… that sounds…" Gerta couldn't quite figure out how to finish the sentence.

"What, that idea never occurred to you before?" Bedford asked.

"Well, I suppose it has. It's just, um…"

"No one has ever put it that bluntly before?" Trudy offered.

"Yes. I suppose that's right," Gerta said. "That's not something you usually think about."

"No, honey," Trudy said gently but firmly. "That's not something *you* usually think about. Other people are forced to think about it all the time."

"Well, I hope you both enjoy living in sin," Bedford said. "The two of you will get what's coming to you when God's judgment comes."

"Bedford, what the fuck is even wrong with you?" Trudy asked. "You actually advocated for the genocide of LGBT people in a country that's not even yours, and somehow you're still able to justify it to yourself."

"It's not genocide, Ms. Hollis. Genocide is when a certain group of people is killed based on something they can't help. You should know this better than most. My understanding is that you were present for the horrors in Rwanda."

Trudy didn't reply to that. She didn't have to.

"But gay people can't help it, either," Gerta said.

"It's a choice," Bedford said. "Don't try to tell me otherwise."

"You honestly think I chose the path that would get me ostracized?" Gerta asked. "You think it makes me happy having to have a sham marriage?"

"Gerta, don't get down and try to argue on his level," Trudy said. "I hate that people like him even act like whether or not it's a choice is the important factor. Love should be love."

Bedford smirked. "So by that definition, you think it's okay for a forty-year-old man to have sex with a twelve-year-old boy if the man says he's in love?"

"Oh, go fuck off, you colossal piece of shit," Trudy said. "If you can't tell the difference between two adults consenting to be with each other and a pedophile forcing themselves on someone too helpless to do anything about it, then you're the one with the sick mind, not us."

Medium Isaiah shouted back at them from the front of the group. "Everyone, be quiet!"

Not only did they stop talking, but they stopped moving. The jungle had become eerily quiet around them, far more than should be natural. It was like all the smaller animals in the trees around them had suddenly fled.

Trudy cautiously made her way to the front of the group and whispered to the Isaiahs. "What is it?"

"There was shaking," Big said. "I felt it."

"Shaking like an earthquake?" Trudy asked. "Is one of the volcanoes in the area acting up?"

"No," Medium said simply. He gave Trudy a long, meaningful look. Trudy thought she knew what that meant.

"Everyone, try to find some place to take cover." Trudy tried to whisper and shout the words at the same time, causing them to come out as neither.

"What is it?" Irving asked.

Trudy didn't need to articulate her theory. There was another shudder in the ground around them, and it most certainly wasn't an earthquake. It lacked the lengthy, sustained rumble that Trudy had felt from the Virungas at times in the past. Instead, this was more like something massive had hit the ground nearby.

"We're about to have company," Trudy said.

For several seconds, there was nothing. Then they heard the roar in the distance that suddenly grew louder with each passing millisecond.

Trudy knew that sound well. She had heard it hundreds of times throughout her life. That was the vocalization of a male silverback gorilla challenging some intruder and thumping its chest.

Except it was much deeper. And growing much, much louder.

"Scatter!" Gerta screamed.

It came down from out of the sky. That fact alone was so

improbable that Trudy's brain got stuck on that for much too long, wondering how it could possibly have done that. For a moment, she completely forgot to be shocked, amazed, and horrified by the gorilla's immense size. It crashed down through the trees a short distance behind them, far enough that no one was immediately crushed but close enough that the shockwave of its impact knocked every member of the party off their feet. That it was, in fact, a fifty-foot-tall gorilla was apparent to all, but Trudy's trained eye, even in those moments of shock, could tell that this was of a species unlike she had ever seen in person. It didn't have the distinctive saddleback of other mountain gorillas, instead standing straighter in an almost human fashion. The shape of its head was slightly different, and its legs were slightly longer and noticeably more muscular.

Jumping, Trudy realized. *That's how it fell from the sky. It can jump unlike any other gorilla ever seen.*

At that thought, the colossal animal launched itself back into the air, almost but not quite straight up. For nearly two seconds, it hung in the air, just long enough for Trudy to realize it was aiming, with unbelievable precision, to come straight back down onto all of them.

"Run!" Trudy screamed. Most of the group managed to stand back up and make a mad dash through the underbrush.

One of them did not.

Trudy looked back just long enough to see that Big Isaiah had gotten his feet tangled in some kind of vine. In any other circumstance, he would have been able to cut through the growth with his machete in no time at all, but he was obviously panicked, and the machete had come out of his hand at some point when he'd fallen. Medium Isaiah, caught up in the flow of the rest of the group, tried to turn around and go back for his brother. Trudy shoved him back along with the others, knowing that because of this he would probably blame her for what was about to happen next. Not that she cared. There was no time to go back for Big Isaiah. Something large blocked out the thin light coming through the canopy directly over him.

Trudy couldn't help but look. Even as she ran, and knowing that was a good way to stumble and break her neck, she had to. It was the scientist in her, the person that had to observe, the one that had to know, no matter how dreadful that knowledge might end up being.

Not that there was much for her to see. A giant gorilla crashed down through the trees, shattering a number of them in the process, and landed directly on top of Big Isaiah. There was a spurt of blood as his body was crushed, yet surprisingly very little that Trudy could see. Just one of the creature's feet was enough to cover the large man completely.

Medium Isaiah screamed for his older brother while Trudy shoved him on, urging everyone to move faster. She didn't dare look back anymore. Something that large could run them down easily in the open, so their only saving grace was the thick forest around them. She had no idea how the gorilla had aimed its jump so precisely to take one of them out, but the canopy above them had to give it some trouble. There was little chance that they'd be able to outrun it in the long run, but it was possible to at least hide.

"We need to find shelter!" Trudy yelled to the others. Somehow, in all the confusion, she had ended up at the front of the group. Medium Isaiah may have been a professional tracker, but obviously, he wasn't going to be at his best at the moment. That meant that Trudy and Gerta were the next in line in terms of the most knowledge of this region, so the group's survival over the next several minutes would hinge upon them.

"We need to get into rockier territory!" Gerta yelled back. "That's our best bet to find caves or overhangs!"

"Rockier territory means less trees!" Trudy yelled back. Behind them, the monster gorilla roared again, added in a few chest thumps, and then took off after them. She could feel the ground shake as it galloped, a sensation punctuated by the destruction of trees. There was no doubt that they were slowing the gorilla down. "The trees are the only thing that's protecting us!"

Another roar behind them, but this time followed by some groaning, crunching sound that Trudy couldn't identify. A few seconds later, though, she understood what it had been as half of an entire tree flew over them, getting close enough that Trudy felt the leaves slice against the top of her head, and smashed into the thicker copse of trees ahead. All of the trees in question exploded in a mass of raining splinters. Everyone had to duck to protect themselves from the debris and shrapnel, forcing them all to grind to a halt.

"Or maybe not," Trudy said. "Head northwest! That way," she said, pointing. "Further up the mountain, there might be some place we can hide!"

They all ran. Bedford glanced over in her direction as he moved. The idea occurred to Trudy that she could trip him right now and leave him for the monster. She didn't do it, but not because of any last minute moment of conscience. She simply thought pausing to do it would slow her down too much.

They kept moving with all their speed, and the sounds behind them said that the giant gorilla was clearly still in pursuit, but it seemed to Trudy that they might be gaining ground. A quick second to look back confirmed this. The gorilla, for all its size, seemed to be getting discouraged as it blundered its way through the jungle. She had no idea how long it would be before the animal made another leap at them.

"Why is it even after us?" Axton asked.

"It senses the wickedness of those among us!" Bedford replied.

"For fuck's sake, Bedford, shut the hell up!" Irving said.

Irving. Suddenly, he seemed like the key here, but Trudy's brain was too oxygen-deprived to properly sort through what it was trying to tell her.

"We're running," Trudy said. "With a normal gorilla, you should never run."

"I'm not sure that we have a choice this time," Irving said.

"Everyone, wait," Trudy said. "Hold up." She stopped, forcing everyone else to stop with her.

"What the hell are you doing?" Axton asked.

"Listen. I don't think it's chasing us anymore." They all listened. The chaotic sounds of a fifty-foot gorilla tearing through the forest after them had subsided.

"My brother," Medium Isaiah said. "That thing killed my brother." He looked like he was ready to go charging back after it with just his machete. Irving put a hand on his chest to stop him.

"I'm sorry, Isaiah. I really am," Irving said. "But for now, we have to concentrate on surviving."

"It shouldn't have come after us," Trudy said, her mind starting to work better now that she had a moment to catch her breath. "Why would it come after us?"

"Obviously, it thought we would be tasty," Bedford said.

"No. It's rare for apes to be carnivorous. When they do eat things other than plants, they're small, like insects, something to supplement their protein."

"In case you didn't notice," Axton said, "it probably does think of us as insects."

"No. That doesn't match anything else we've seen so far regarding food sources. There has to be another reason for it to attack."

"The only other people we know that it's attacked so far are poachers," Gerta said.

"So why would it equate us with poachers?" Trudy asked. She looked at each one of the people in the party in turn, then looked back at Irving and stared for a long time.

"Shit," Trudy finally said. "It's so obvious."

Irving's face fell as he too understood. Before anyone else could ask what Trudy meant, he shrugged off his backpack and started rooting around for it.

"Seriously?" Axton asked. "That thing is trying to kill us because we took a rock?"

Irving removed the stone from the sample bag. "How does he even know where the stone is?"

"We don't know that it's a he," Trudy said absently as she took a closer look at the stone. The closer she got, the more it curled her nose hairs.

"Would a female be that aggressive?" Gerta asked.

"Probably not. So yeah, it probably is male, but we can't be sure." With her face practically resting on the crudely carved ape, Trudy took a deep whiff.

"What are you doing?" Irving asked.

"The smell. That's how he's tracking us," Trudy said. "Go ahead, sniff it."

Irving did as she said and scrunched up his nose. "Why didn't I smell that before?"

"To be fair, when most people come across the scientific find of a lifetime, it's not usually their highest priority to stick their nose in it," Trudy said.

"What is it?" Gerta asked before making her own sniff. "It's faint but... is that urine?"

Trudy nodded. "One of the gorillas pissed on it. Marked it. A normal mountain gorilla wouldn't have a powerful enough sense of smell to track it, but something like our new friend? We don't have any clue what he might be capable of."

"So all we should need to do is set the stone down, then get the hell out of here before that thing comes to get it, right?" Axton asked.

"Well, we sure as hell shouldn't keep carrying it around with us," Trudy said. "Ideally, I'd say we should put it back where we found it, but I kind of doubt he would let us go right back to the site without smashing us."

"Do you hear something again?" Bedford asked.

"No," Trudy said out of habit. Whatever Bedford said, she just wanted to instinctively disagree. But as soon as the word was out of her mouth, she realized it wasn't true. Somewhere back along the way they had come, she thought she heard a massive amount of rustling.

"Irving, put the stone down now and run!" Trudy said. He dropped it, and Trudy saw a small piece chip off. Then they all scattered, getting out of the way just seconds before the gorilla again dropped down from the sky directly behind where they'd just been standing.

"No, wait, stop!" Gerta yelled at them. "Stay absolutely still!"

Trudy was about to argue before she remembered that Gerta was right. Running would only get him to chase them again. "Take a knee!" Trudy said. "Don't look him in the face! Be submissive!"

They were spread out enough that it was difficult for Trudy to be sure if everyone did as she said. Medium certainly hesitated the longest, his hand still tightly gripping his machete, but he too did his best to show the giant gorilla that it was superior to him. Now it was just a moment of wait and see. Either he would acknowledge their acquiescence, or else he would slaughter them all before they could think about moving again.

The entire forest became still and silent. Trudy barely dared to breathe out of fear that than any movement at all might be taken as a challenge. Her lungs still burned from the run, and her body shook from both terror and the continued effects of not having any alcohol, but she forced everything about herself to be still. The only thing that wouldn't stop was her mind, which raced with thoughts completely out of control.

Oh my God look at the coloring, is that red I see in his coat? Interesting, the color and coat suggest maybe some kind of orangutan DNA and yet he's still clearly a gorilla, oh God he's going to kill us all please let the others go, okay you can kill Bedford if that's what you want, but the others need to go, oh please let Gerta live, I don't want to watch her die, I kind of love her even though I don't, kill me instead I deserve it, I deserve it so much for what happened with Killroy, please just kill me, please just get it over with, please let Gerta go, please, please, please...

She risked looking up ever so slightly. Trudy knew it was a risk, but she still had to see. He was truly magnificent, and yet still terrifying. It wasn't just his size, but the fact that he existed at all. No giant gorilla in any fiction, from King Kong to Mighty Joe Young to fucking Donkey Kong, could possibly give any hint as to the majesty of this massive creature. His chest heaved as he breathed, and his head twisted this way and that as he examined the tiny creatures in front of him that had dared desecrate the gorilla graveyard. What was he thinking? Trudy wondered. Did he hate them? Pity them? Did he even recognize them as something that could think, or were they just far inferior version of himself, like humans might think of pygmy monkeys?

Trudy was torn between her every instinct as a scientist—to study him, to catalogue him, to give him reason and meaning—and her survival instincts as a creature clearly lower in the chain of life. She could see how other gorillas might come to see him as a god. A deep-seated part of her even wanted to do that herself.

He made a series of snorts and snuffles as he looked around at them all. With a few lumbering steps, he came closer to Bedford, who himself now looked like he was bowing and praying before a deity. Trudy held her breath as the gorilla reached out gently nudged Bedford. Bedford only barely kept his balance. Even with his head down, Trudy could tell from his soft sniffling and the occasional full-body sob that he was crying, probably believing that this was indeed it, this was the moment he was going to die.

The gorilla made an abrupt, coughing vocalization, then moved away from him.

Trudy let out her breath. She'd seen this kind of thing in normal mountain gorillas. He was accepting their show of submissiveness. If he hadn't tried to kill the rest of them by now, then he wasn't going to at all.

His enormous nostrils flared as he barked a startled, almost angry-sounding cry. Trudy held her breath again. Maybe she had been wrong.

The gorilla reached down for the small stone statue where Irving had dropped it. It was so tiny compared to him, like if Trudy were to hold a sesame seed. Would he notice the small part that had broken off, or was such a detail too little for him to take notice?

He held it up to his nose. He sniffed it several times.

Then he roared. It was a monstrous, deafening cry that echoed out through the entire jungle around them, shaking the leaves on the trees with its power. With stunning speed, he spun around in a circle, deeply taking in the scent of every member of the group.

He stopped for only just a second in front of Irving before he ripped the man in half.

It all happened so quickly, a blur of blood and guts and gore as the gorilla dropped the stone, no longer seeming to care about it one way or the other, and grabbed Irving with both hands. The two mighty paws covered Irving completely, drowning out any attempt the man might have made to scream for help. The creature lifted Irving in the air even as he pulled his arms apart, keeping hold of everything below Irving's waist with one and Irving's torso with the other. Blood spurted all over Trudy along with some meaty chunk that might have been part of Irving's intestine, although Trudy's mind shut down just enough that it wouldn't let her realize that until later.

The gorilla held up the two halves of Trudy's former employer to the sky, and the sound that came from his mouth could only be described as a scream of triumph.

His legs bunched then pushed him off the ground. He leaped up into the sky and vanished. Several seconds later, Trudy heard the earth-rumbling thump as the gorilla landed some distance away. She continued listening for the sounds of its jumps and landings until she was absolutely, one hundred percent sure the gorilla wasn't coming back.

Then she collapsed to the ground and puked all over herself.

CHAPTER TEN:
HOLLIS IN THE VIRUNGAS

As Trudy's mind once again started working properly in registering the here and now, the first thing she became aware of was the ghastly stink emanating from the front of her button-up shirt. Not only did it now hold the remains of her breakfast, but there were several stinking, steaming pieces that might have been parts of Irving's bowls.

I bet he'd sell his soul for real to get that back in him, am I right? Trudy thought incongruously. The black humor set her to retching again, but there was nothing to come up now. Once her stomach was back under her control, she hastily wiped as much of the mess off her front as she could, then shakily stood up to look for the others.

The other four remaining members of their team were a tableau of the wide variety of ways humans reacted to something terrible. Medium Isaiah (*I guess we can just call him Isaiah now*, the black humorist in her said) was on his knees weeping profusely, a strange sight in such a large man, and yet Trudy would have expected nothing else from him. Bedford had toppled over in what might have been a faint, although he was stirring and moaning as though in the middle of a bad dream. Axton stood completely frozen in place, his gaze locked in the direction the giant gorilla had gone. Trudy had to look closely just to be sure he was breathing. Out of all of them, Gerta looked like she was the one who had herself the most together. Although clearly shaking, she moved among each of the others, checking on them, making sure there wasn't any kind of medical trauma that needed to be addressed. These were the actions of someone who had seen plenty of horrible things in the past and knew how to compartmentalize them. Later, maybe, Gerta would break down. For now, though, she saw that no one else was yet capable of taking the lead, which made her the current leader by default.

"Everyone, get up," Gerta said. "We need to move."

"This can't be real," Axton whispered. Gerta went over to him, looked him deep in the eyes for a moment, and the slapped him across the cheek.

"Ow! Shit! What did you do that for?" Axton asked as he rubbed his face.

"I said we need to move," Gerta said. "No waiting. He might come back for us."

This caught everyone's attention. Personally, Trudy didn't think the gorilla would return, but she had no other behavioral patterns to base this thing's actions on. It may have looked very much like a gorilla, but the differences were not just in its size. Its actions with Irving had been hyper-aggressive in a way she had only seen with the most abused animals. They could make no assumptions on what it would or wouldn't do.

Irving's pack sat on the ground near where he'd stood. He'd never had a chance to put it back on after removing the stone sculpture, which means the party still had it and all its contents. Trudy felt slightly ghoulish grabbing the pack and awkwardly shifting it into position on her back next to her own. She almost felt she should leave it in the same way she had wanted to leave the six stones sitting unmolested, as a marker to a violent death. But they needed the supplies inside. For all they knew, their survival now could depend on it.

The thought of the stones made Trudy turn back and look for the sculpture. It took her several seconds of searching in the trampled underbrush, mostly because it was well and thoroughly shattered now.

Just like Turtle herself, Trudy thought. Her next thought was that she shouldn't still be mourning an animal that was over twenty-years dead when there were the remains of humans still scattered all about her. Yet that was the way her brain worked sometimes. Sometimes the humans felt like the animals, and the animals felt more human.

Her mind tried to take her back to the incident at the Cooper Memorial Zoo. She physically shook the thought off and away. No time for that. No time for anything but finding a safe place to hide. The sky was starting to grow darker, and none of them wanted to still be out in the open once they could no longer see what might be coming for them.

Bedford was the hardest to get moving again. Just standing alone seemed to be hard for him. He didn't have the same vacant stare as Axton or the tear-streaked cheeks of Isaiah, though. There was something distinctly disturbing in the way he looked ahead of himself, as though he could now see something no one else could, and it both frightened and exhilarated him. Trudy shoved him to move forward, and their dwindled group once more set out. They didn't run now, but neither did they dare dawdle. Gerta took the lead, with Axton, Isaiah, and Bedford behind her. Trudy took the rear position, knowing that next to Gerta, she was probably the one in the best condition to keep an eye or ear out for any sign of the monster gorilla's return.

For nearly an hour they walked in tense silence. Trudy almost wanted to ask Gerta where exactly she was leading them, but she already thought she knew the answer: Gerta didn't have the slightest clue. She was just leading them in a general direction that was away from the carnage they had just witnessed. The woman could be leading them back to civilization or further away, yet no one cared to find out for sure. Again, there would be time for that kind of thought later, once they were safe for the night. If, that was, safety was even still something any of them could have out here.

Finally, they found a rocky overhang coming out of the steep side of a ridge. Trudy glanced over it for a few minutes before determining that this was probably the best they were going to get for the night. It was high up enough that they wouldn't have to worry about flash flooding, just barely flat enough to set up a couple of the tents, and the overhang would hopefully prove to be a small enough space for them to avoid the enormous grasping hands of the gorilla, if it came to that. Gerta directed them in setting up the camp. Isaiah started to gather sticks for a fire, but Trudy stopped him quickly. They didn't want anything to act as a beacon announcing where they were. Isaiah simply nodded and sat on the ground, giving up at all attempts at work. Bedford was equally useless, while Axton at least had enough sense back that he could be directed to do a few simple tasks. The women took charge, and none of the three men protested.

Time became a blur to Trudy for a while after they had a rudimentary camp set up and darkness fell on them. They'd only been able to set up two of the tents, as the third had been among Big Isaiah's supplies and were now likely smashed permanently into the forest floor. Isaiah and Axton took one tent while Trudy and Gerta took the other. Axton offered Bedford a place in theirs, but he quietly shook his head. He hadn't actually said anything at all since the incident, and his quiet made Trudy uneasy. Instead of going into the tent, Bedford found a blanket and wrapped it tightly around himself as he huddled in the far corner of rocks under the overhang. There was no way that was a comfortable sleeping position, but Trudy couldn't argue that it was likely the safest place in the whole camp.

Once Trudy and Gerta were together in the tent, there was an awkward moment where Trudy thought them both might take solace in each other's bodies, but any time Trudy touched Gerta, all she could feel was the warm, wet viscera raining down on her from what used to be Irving. Trudy couldn't bring herself to have any contact with Gerta for a while after that, and they went to sleep without doing anything more than telling each other that that they would see them in the morning.

Halfway through the night, Trudy woke to find Gerta curled up against her and crying softly. Trudy just held her until they were both asleep again.

In the light of morning, Trudy couldn't help but feel like the energy in the camp was incredibly weird. They all got up and started about morning chores and duties like nothing had happened the day before. The only noticeable difference was that they were now short two pairs of hands. Isaiah had gained back enough of himself that he was able to go off briefly to hunt. He came back with a dik-dik, a small deer-like creature native to this region, and they did their best to prepare it with the smallest possible fire. Once they were all around each other again and had food in their bellies, it became obvious that nothing more could happen until they had a good, long talk.

"The very first thing we need to do is decide where we're going," Trudy said.

"Um, I think that should be pretty easy," Axton said. "We head back to Kabale. Right? I mean, you can't honestly say that you want to continue on with the expedition after what happened."

"That would absolutely be my first instinct," Trudy said. "If, you know, there wasn't a giant motherfucking gorilla between there and us."

"Hold on," Gerta said, taking time to pull out their map. "Well, there's a number of small villages we could try to reach instead that would be much, much closer than Kabale. But I'm not sure we really want to do that."

"Why not?" Axton asked.

"Because we can't be sure that gorilla isn't going to follow us," Trudy said.

"Didn't he get what he wanted?" Bedford asked. "He killed the person who desecrated his sacred site, and the stone got smashed in the process."

Something about the words he used disturbed Trudy. Previously, he had been completely dismissive of the stones and the kill site as anything worth noting or preserving. Now all of a sudden it was a "sacred site?" Just what exactly was going on in this guy's head?

"We don't know that for sure," Trudy said. "It could be that he just took a break before he intends to come after the rest of us. And if he does intend to get us, then we would be leading him right into a bunch of other people. They would get slaughtered."

"But we might have other people to help us then," Axton said. "They could call in the military..."

"That is stupid," Isaiah said. "A small village is not going to be able to get help from the military. I think you have the wrong idea about how the military actually works in African countries."

Axton looked away.

"Look, for the safety of others, we should make sure that he isn't going to come after us before we get any innocents involved," Gerta said.

"So what other options does that leave us?" Bedford asked. "Are you saying that we need to just camp in the wilderness until we are sure we haven't been marked?"

"We could do that," Trudy said, "or we could continue on with our original plan. Go deeper. Find this mysterious food source. Unravel the mystery."

"I can't believe this," Axton said. "You *are* saying we should go on as though nothing happened."

"It's all probably a moot point at the moment, anyway," Gerta said. "We got pretty turned around while we were running. We can't be sure we are exactly where we should be at this point. Before we can make any decision about which way to go in the long run, we first have to find some marker or landmark that tells us where we actually are in the forest. Because it actually looks to me like we may have crossed the border out of Bwindi and Uganda, and into the Democratic Republic of the Congo."

"Fuck," Trudy said. "If that's the case, we may not even want to have contact with anyone. We're not supposed to be here. If some random person with an itchy trigger finger finds us and tries to ask us for official papers, it likely won't matter which country we originally come from. It's easy to hide a body in the jungle."

Gerta cocked her head at the map, then looked at a compass she had pulled out. "So I think our best idea right now is to head directly north. If we are already in the DRC, then we will not really be heading any deeper in. Instead, we will be walking parallel to the border. If we are still in Uganda, then we do not risk accidentally crossing the border. Once we have gone far enough that we think our gorilla friend is not going to follow us, then we can turn and head due east. It's possible there's a seasonal road in that area, and if we stumble across it, then we can follow it to the village of Bulema."

"I suppose that's as good of a plan as any," Trudy said.

"Could you do me a favor, though?" Axton asked Gerta. "Could you please not refer to that thing as our friend? I already had a friend on this trip. He may have been my employer as well, but he was still a friend. And now he's ripped into pieces. Nothing that does that is my friend."

"It's not like we have much else to call him," Gerta asked. "We don't even know for sure what he is. Or even that he is a he."

Bedford looked at Trudy. "You're supposed to be the expert.

Do you have any ideas?"

Trudy shrugged. "Couldn't tell you. There is evidence in the fossil record of great apes that are significantly larger than what we currently know, but not like that."

"How much is significantly larger?" Axton asked.

"The largest recorded ape in the known fossil record is a specimen called *Gigantopithecus blacki*. Unfortunately, we know next to nothing about what it might have looked like. The only fossils that have ever been found are a couple of jaw bones, which obviously doesn't give scientists much to go on. Based on the proportions, though, it was probably about ten feet high."

Gerta cocked her head, amused despite herself. "Which would be what, exactly, to everyone here that doesn't use ridiculously outdated measurement systems?"

"Three meters or so. So obviously there's a big difference between that and what we're seeing here. And besides, based on the fact that those fossils were found in East Asia, it seems much more likely that *G. blacki* had more in common with the modern orangutan than it would with gorillas."

"Still, we have no better name for it," Axton said. "So I vote for Gigantocus."

Trudy shrugged. "Whatever. I guess."

Gerta twirled a lock of her hair absently in thought. "Let's say for a minute that Gigantocus was some relative of *G. blacki*. What would that tell us about him?"

"Again, we've only ever seen the jaw bone, so not much, but what we would know comes back to the same thing I've already been saying over and over. Food source. *G. blacki* is believed to have gone extinct because it had a highly specialized diet. And when that diet could no longer be found in its environment, it died out."

"Hmm," Gerta said, once again looking at the map. "If we have indeed crossed over into the DCR, then it seems more likely that we might stumble onto such a food source here. There is far less development on that side of the border, so there are lots of places for previously undiscovered things to still be hiding."

"Look, we're not continuing the expedition," Axton said. "Irving was the one employing you all. Now that he's gone, I guess that mean I have the purse strings. I'm pulling the plug on all of this."

"Fine," Gerta said. "So is there anything else we need to discuss?"

"How about we discuss what this all really means?" Bedford asked.

"I get the distinct impression that I don't actually want to ask you what you're talking about," Trudy said. "Just like I get the impression that you're going to tell us anyway."

"While I was sleeping last night, God came to me."

Trudy, Gerta, Axton, and even Isaiah all exchanged uneasy expressions.

"Bedford, we don't have time for this," Gerta said.

"Don't you understand?" Bedford asked. "I was wrong all along."

Trudy snorted. "Hell, I've been saying that since the moment I first knew you even existed."

"You may joke, Ms. Hollis, but after the unfortunate death of Mr. Irving and our guide, God put scales over my eyes, like Paul on the road to Damascus."

"He was still Saul on the way to Damascus, you dumbass," Trudy said. "Get your Bible stories straight."

Bedford ignored her. "I was stricken. I did not know what to do. But last night, the Lord came to me in a dream. He told me what must happen next."

"And what, exactly, was that?" Axton asked.

Bedford looked around at them as though he only just now realized he wasn't preaching to the most receptive audience. "Perhaps it would be best if I kept his plan a secret for now."

"Mr. Bedford, please stop acting like you are the only Christian here," Isaiah said. "I may not have believed as fervently as my brother, but I am still a follower. And I do not believe you."

"Neither do the other Christians here," Gerta said. She held up her hand to indicate that she was among that group. Trudy reluctantly held up her hand as well. Axton was the only one who refrained. "You do not speak for us."

Bedford raised an eyebrow. Trudy could already guess that he didn't consider any of them true followers of his faith at all, but she didn't give a rat's ass what he thought. Trudy knew who and what she was.

"If we're done playing Bedford's damned mind games, maybe we should pack up and get going?" Axton asked. "No matter what happens next, it looks like we've got a long journey still ahead of us."

Axton wasn't kidding. They followed Gerta's direction, since she was the one with both a compass and the map, and the route didn't take them anywhere near humanity for the entire day. The actual distance they travelled couldn't have been more than five miles as the bird flies, but the majority of it was up and down mountains. While both Axton and Bedford had found their second wind for a while in the morning, they quickly ran out and slowed the group down again. For all their complaining, and for all the danger they were probably still in, Trudy almost found herself having fun. It reminded her of her earlier days, back before this region of the world had been as well mapped, back when every corner they turned could result in some new subspecies of animal that she hadn't seen before. At one point, she saw a boomslang slither rather close to Bedford, its bright green coloring hiding the highly poisonous snake for quite some time. She didn't bother to tell him that, although she didn't let him walk right into it, either. Instead, she found a large stick and pushed it gently aside before Bedford even realized he had been in danger.

You're getting soft, Hollis, Trudy thought.

They took frequent breaks, and for both lunch and dinner, Isaiah went out hunting long enough to bring them something back, once another dik-dik and the other time something that might have been a mongoose before Isaiah had hacked it up. As night approached again, nobody spoke around the fire. They at least felt comfortable now having a fire, as long as they kept it small, since they hadn't seen any sign at all that Gigantocus was still following them. Axton did sing something softly, though, and everyone stopped to listen. He had a surprisingly melodious voice. If he ever decided to no longer be a paid lackey and yes-man, he might actually have a career in music.

Trudy almost said so out loud, before she remembered that the person here most likely to have connections to the music industry was now just a pile of guts somewhere behind them.

Trudy retired to their tent first, hoping that she would be asleep and untempted by Gerta by the time the other joined her, but Gerta came in soon after. Gerta gave her an expression that seemed part come-hither and part sheer exhaustion.

"I'd almost think you were trying to avoid me by going to bed so early," Gerta said softly.

Trudy's first impulse was to lie. After a few seconds thought, though, she said, "That's exactly what I was doing."

"May I ask why?"

"It's... difficult to explain."

"Trudy, it's probably not that difficult. I bet I can even guess. You know longer care what Bedford thinks, and you want me."

"Um, yeah..."

"But at the same time, doing anything of the sort would feel too morbid, wouldn't it?" Gerta asked. "Like we have no right to have sex after what we saw yesterday."

Trudy nodded. "And yet at the same time, I kind of want to do it even more..."

"...because you just want to prove that you're still alive. Am I right?"

"Pretty close. Honestly, Gerta, that's a bit creepy."

"What is?"

"The way you seemed to just know my thoughts."

Gerta shrugged. She sat down on a blanket next to Trudy so that the two of them were almost, but not quite, touching.

"I just know you."

"Not really, you don't. We had a fling a long time ago back when you were young enough that something between us shouldn't have been appropriate. Just because we've seen each other on occasion since then doesn't mean we've developed some kind of connection."

"Maybe we have. How would you know? You always seem to be running from any kind of connection at all."

Trudy would have been almost insulted by that if it hadn't been so close to the truth. "Can you blame me? I did have what I thought was a deep, lasting connection with someone once. Everyone knows how that turned out."

"No, not everyone," Gerta said. She paused for a long moment before finally saying. "If you would like to talk about it, I would like to listen. Or if you don't, we can get on to something else."

"Like screwing like bunnies?"

Gerta chuckled. "Or sleep. We do still have people in the other tent that would hear us."

"They're adults. I'm pretty sure they would have heard people having sex by now."

"Not two women, maybe."

"Axton's not going to care."

Gerta bit her lip thoughtfully. "No, I don't think he would. Bedford, however…"

"I don't give a shit what Bedford thinks anymore. I don't think he was all there to start with, and I definitely don't think he's all there now. You heard the way he was talking today."

"I was thinking also of Isaiah."

"Really? You think he would have a problem with us?"

"You haven't spent as much time in Uganda recently as I have. Lots of people take a live and let live policy when it comes to same-sex relations around here, not at all like the media might have you believe. Unless you're doing something that they perceive to be shoving it in their face."

"Not that I give a rat's ass what he would think, Gerta."

"Maybe not, but don't forget that I don't have the luxury of not caring," Gerta said. "My work frequently takes me back here."

"Hmph," Trudy said in a non-committed fashion. She started to turn away from Gerta in an effort to try sleeping, then thought for a moment and turned back. "You know, I never did talk to anybody about what happened with Barbara."

"You know, I think that might be the first time I've even heard you use your ex-wife's name." The two of them lay down next to each other in much the same way they did the other night, positioned so that they could both face each other, but for some reason, this instance didn't have the same level of sexual tension. "Otherwise, I've just know that her last name was Nelson. And that's only because you hyphenated your name for a while."

"I guess there's not a lot to tell," Trudy said. "We were in love for a while. Then we weren't. I was fine with that. She wasn't. She also had a secret gambling problem, apparently, and she funded it by embezzling from our Hollis-Nelson Foundation. And then she found someone else. All that came to light one day when I walked in on them."

"But where did this happen?"

"The bedroom at my condo. Although, I guess at the time it was the bedroom of our condo."

"The bedroom you shared together? Really?"

Trudy sighed and looked away for a moment. "Yes. Really."

"That seems especially disrespectful."

"What, you've never had sex with another woman in your husband's bed?"

"Now that's neither fair nor the same thing, and you know it. I almost think you are trying to piss me off to get this conversation to end."

Trudy looked back at her. "Maybe. You're probably right. I wouldn't have been so ham-handed with the attempt if I'd had something to drink."

"Going back to when you walked in on your wife with another woman, though…"

"Do we really have to go back to it?"

"You can end the conversation any time you wish, Trudy. Just say so."

Trudy thought about it for a while before softly replying, "No. Go ahead."

"I would almost think that, in that situation, it was as if she wanted you to find out."

"Yeah, I'm pretty sure she did. She didn't want to keep lying to me, and she was ashamed of what she had been doing with our charitable organization, but she didn't want to directly come out and tell me, either. I suppose I don't blame her. I'm a total bitch when I'm angry. This way she at least had the element of surprise against me."

"So you two got divorced?"

"Yep. I wish I could say there was more to the story than that. Or maybe I just wish that we hadn't let it go on that long. We knew we were wrong for each other. But we'd talked for so long about getting married that, by the time it was finally legal for us, it was more of a symbol than anything else. I honestly think I was already falling out of love with her at the time. She just wasn't..."

Trudy didn't continue until Gerta physically prodded her to keep going. "Just wasn't what?"

"This is going to sound really fucking stupid. I mean, incredibly stupid. Like, something is seriously wrong with me stupid."

"Go ahead. I promise not to laugh much," Gerta said lightly, but her face was serious. No, Trudy knew, Gerta was certainly not going to laugh at all.

"She wasn't a gorilla."

Gerta blinked at her several times. "Excuse me?"

"Wait, you know what? You can probably interpret that wrong, like I actually wanted to sleep with a gorilla. What I meant was, she wasn't a part of my work. She didn't have any relationship to it at all. We were more of a scientist super-couple than anything, something the papers saw and liked to play up. Putting our names together was a good way to get rich people to donate money for various scientific research. But my time in the Virungas when I was younger, they changed me. I couldn't make anything else a part of my life. My work was how I defined myself. And then it all crashed down when..."

Trudy stopped herself. No. She couldn't talk about this. No one could ever know, especially not Gerta.

"Trudy?" Gerta said. "What is it?"

"Nothing."

"You were about to discuss what happened with Killroy."

"You already know what happened, Gerta. There's no point in going over it again."

"Trudy." Gerta reached out in the growing darkness of their tent and took Trudy's hand. "I know there has to be something you didn't tell me. It's okay. I can listen."

No. Not this. Trudy couldn't tell her this. She couldn't tell anyone. She had to die with this secret. She had to drink herself into oblivion because of it.

"I've tried not to pry," Gerta said. "But this has obviously destroyed you. Warped you. Whatever detail you left out, it's going to continue eating you until you tell someone. If not me, then you have to find someone else. Because I don't want to keep seeing you in pain like this."

"I'm not in pain." Even to Trudy's own ears, the words didn't sound at all convincing.

"Okay, then," Gerta said. She turned over so her back was facing Trudy. "I'll leave it be."

The tent grew quiet. For nearly ten minutes, Trudy continued to lie on her back, staring up at the top of the tent. Finally, in a voice so low even she could barely hear it, she said, "Gerta? Are you   asleep?"
Gerta said nothing, but Trudy could tell from her breathing that she was still awake.

"You're asleep," Trudy said softly. "I'm going to tell you my secret, and you won't hear it, got it? You won't hear any of it, and I will never have any reason to believe you did hear it. Do you understand?"

Of course, Gerta couldn't actually answer, but Trudy detected a slight shudder of her hair that she thought was a nod. Or maybe she had been wrong. Maybe Gerta really was asleep and that movement had just been her unconsciously shifting to get more comfortable.

That's what I choose to believe, Trudy said. *She won't hear any of this.*

"Killroy was my friend."

Trudy paused for a very long time here. She could barely even see Gerta's form directly in front of her, the tent had grown so dark. She listened to Gerta's breathing, waiting for the moment when she was sure that Gerta really had fallen asleep, if she wasn't already. But she couldn't be sure. She didn't even want to be sure. Somehow, this was the only way she could make her confession. She had to be as unsure as possible that she was even confessing to anyone at all.

"That's something no one seems to get. The news pundits, the assholes in their mom's basements making memes of me and him, the armchair warriors that all have their own completely uneducated opinion about the day I killed him. They don't get that I fed him. I played with him. I bathed him. I went with him on every trip where they sent him around to other zoos in an attempt to get him to breed in captivity. The people who talk about this, they make a joke of him. But he was more real to me than most humans are. For fuck's sake, no one even knows, but he hugged me when I got divorced. He saw me crying, knew I was in distress, and did that thing he always saw humans do when they wanted to comfort each other. Can you imagine what that must have looked like? A huge, fully grown, male silverback mountain gorilla lumbering up to me and awkwardly putting an arm around me? He made little vocalizations. He was honestly trying to be soothing. No one else knew that about him. No one.

"But even though he was more like people to me than actual people, he was still a gorilla. He still had gorilla instincts. A lot of noise has been made about his actions when that little girl fell into his enclosure. The people who say I had no right to shoot him, they say that he was acting to protect her, that he obviously thought of her as just another little gorilla that was part of his group. These are the same fuckers that think they know everything about science just because they like a Facebook page about it. They don't know shit. Reading one article doesn't make them an expert. I'm the expert. I'm the one who spent all my life following gorillas through the Virungas. I'm the one who was with Killroy at all times. And I knew. I saw the way he was dragging her. Killroy was agitated. He'd been in captivity so long that all he knew was routine, and this sudden alien presence in his enclose was against routine. Without routine, he fell back to his instincts. He dragged her around the enclosure not the way he would a baby gorilla, but the way he would something that was invading his territory. He was frightened. I know it sounds idiotic, a six-foot gorilla scared of a toddler, but he was.

"The people who say I did the wrong thing, they say I should have waited, that he wouldn't have hurt her. But I knew. I couldn't wait. She was too small. The way Killroy pulled her around, it would break her. So I ran into our emergency supplies and got a rifle that we had on hand just in case of this exact problem. I had no problem bringing the butt up to my shoulder. I had no problem looking through the scope."

Trudy stopped. She didn't have to continue. There was no way Gerta was still awake. Trudy could just turn over herself, go to sleep, and forget that she had ever started this. But at no point since Killroy's death had she said any of this out loud, not even to herself. She needed to hear the words. Maybe saying it would make her feel less evil. Maybe when it was put into language rather than the raw feelings coursing through her mind, she would see it differently. It might no longer feel so bad.

Actually, that was why she wanted to stop. She didn't want the pain and guilt to go away. Some part of her wanted it to stay, wanted it to be the excuse for why she drank. She wanted an easy reason to hate herself instead of having to sit and seriously consider her messed up psychology.

Gerta mumbled in her sleep, or at least it could have been a mumble. I could have also been Gerta's quiet way of telling her to continue, that she would listen no matter what, that she wouldn't judge. Trudy turned her back to the woman, no longer able to sit and see all the signs that she either was or wasn't sleeping.

Trudy took a deep breath.

"None of the cameras saw. I watched every single video afterward. I looked at all the security footage, even the ones that were never released to the public. I searched through YouTube, ignoring all the hateful comments so that I could look at every single bit of camera phone footage that had been posted from that day. And none of them caught it. None of them saw the moment. It was just me. I'm the only one who knew what happened in that instant. All they show is me aiming, taking a long time to line up the shot, and then firing. They didn't see what I saw."

A hand slithered over Trudy and held her tightly. Was Gerta awake and acknowledging that she was listening, or had this been the unconscious gesture of someone seeking warmth as they dreamed? Trudy's voice became so low that she could barely even hear herself.

"I looked through the scope. I knew I had to shoot. I aimed the sights at Killroy. I knew what I had to do. But I remembered that hug he gave me. In that moment, I tried to doubt that it was in fact a hug, that it was just some gorilla thing that I had misinterpreted, but my brain was convinced. I knew I was about to shoot my last friend. I had to do it. And it made me angry. I was furious that I had been put into this situation. My mind wasn't working right from the anger. And in that anger, I suddenly found myself blaming that little girl. I hated her. She was only two or three, she'd done nothing wrong, but I hated her. I hated her parents that had let her out of their sight long enough for her to climb over the fence. I hated whatever piece of shit had improperly designed the fence in the first place. I hated everyone and everything. I hated all of humanity for putting me in this position.

"So I moved the sights on the scope. Instead of targeting Killroy, I moved it so I was targeting that little girl's head."

Gerta made a soft gasp. The illusion was gone. She was listening. She had listened to it all. Trudy wanted to get up and run off to the jungle, as far away as possible from Gerta's inevitable judgment, yet the worst detail was already out. There was no taking any of the story back. She had to see it through to the end.

"I didn't know how long at the time that I sat there with that little girl in my sights, my finger on the trigger, ready to squeeze and end the whole stupid thing. I think maybe there was a vague idea in my head that, as soon as I did it, I would turn the gun on myself. There was enough ammo for it, and despite the awkward angle, I was pretty sure I could do it fast enough that no one would stop me. It would be like a punishment to the human race, you see. Humans had taken Kramer and the rest of his group from me, along with so many other gorillas that I had met and known in my travels, that this would be like payback. You took my children from me, humans, so now I'm going to take yours.

"Through that scope, I could see the girl's face so clearly. I could see the terror. I knew it should have stopped me, that I should have had enough natural human empathy that I would be appalled by even considering such a thing, but all I could think about was Turtle. I thought about the way the poachers had hacked her up for no apparent reason, like it had been so much fun for them. Maybe I could have that fun, too, maybe that would be the true revenge. That I enjoyed it."

Trudy took another deep breath. "And that was when I came back to myself. It was such a long moment in my head, yet only took up a few seconds on the videos. Something else took over, some part of me that I've been trying to understand ever since and still can't figure out to this day. It was as if someone inside me, someone who was a much better person than I could ever be, gently nudged the weapon back into place so I was sighting Killroy again. And before I could change my mind, before I could let that dark and vengeful part of me have control again, I fired. The shot was perfect. It hit Killroy directly between the eyes. He fell, and I fled. I didn't even wait to see if the girl was okay. I couldn't face her, and I certainly couldn't face any other human. Instead, I found a bottle that I had stashed in a hidden place in my office, and I finished the whole thing in one go."

Trudy turned over to face Gerta. Despite the darkness, it was impossible not to see that her eyes were open. They shimmered slightly with tears, but other than that, there was nothing to show any expression on her face.

"So now you know," Trudy said. "That's it. That's my deep dark secret."

"Trudy," Gerta said softly.

"If you don't even want to be in the same tent with me anymore, I'll understand," Trudy said. "I can get out and sleep in the open."

"Trudy, you didn't do it."

"But that's not the point. I almost did. I wanted to. I could have."

"But you didn't."

"You know, this was a mistake." Trudy started to get up so she could leave. Gerta's hand firmly grasped her shoulder and kept her from getting up.

"Let me go," Trudy whispered.

"No. Trudy, listen to me. Look me in the eyes and really listen to me. You. Didn't. Kill. The girl."

Trudy looked away. "You still don't get it."

"Then try to explain it."

"Don't you see? There's still a part of me that wished I did it. Because then my friend would still be alive."

Trudy turned over again. Her whole body instinctively curled into a ball as the tears came, forcing her to shake uncontrollably with the sobs.

Through it all, Gerta still held her tight. Like this, Trudy was finally able to fall asleep.

CHAPTER ELEVEN:
FOLLOW THE LEADER

While Gerta still seemed to be acting as the leader and only person that she knew what she was doing, Isaiah seemed mostly back to his old self as they continued on, at least in terms of his tracking. That was why they let him slip off by himself for a while in the afternoon as Gerta stopped to take stock once more of their position.

"Look. See? I think we're right here," Gerta said, pointing to a raised ridge on the map just over the border into the Democratic Republic of the Congo. "I think this is that ridge right over there." She pointed at a noticeable landmark nearby.

Trudy took a closer look at the map. It was difficult for her to meet Gerta's gaze today, even though she knew it shouldn't have been. Gerta had said nothing this morning. It truly was like she had been asleep the whole time, and Trudy almost wondered for real if Gerta's soothing words had been part of a dream. She doubted it, of course, but neither could she imagine Gerta not hating her this morning. If Gerta truly didn't hate her for her admission, then maybe that could go some distance to Trudy no longer hating herself.

"Well, if that's right, then we have two options as I see it," Trudy said. Axton was hovering nearby, silently watching and listening to everything they said. Bedford wandered off about ten feet from them as though he were looking for something in the trees above him. That was probably dangerous, given how little he knew about survival around here, but Trudy wasn't going to waste their precious time calling him back. Trudy put her own finger on the map. "If we keep going straight north, we'll hit this road. It's probably disused, but it's our best chance for being found by someone. The problem with that, of course…"

"Is that whoever we might meet on the road will be from the DRC," Gerta finished for her. "The road eventually goes back over the border into Uganda, and then eventually, we'll hit Bulema."

"What's the other option?" Axton asked.

"We go straight east," Trudy said. "Now that we know where we are, we know exactly how far it is to the border. We'll be out of the DRC quickly and won't have to deal with any possible international entanglements."

"Why don't you sound too enthusiastic about that option?" Axton asked.

Gerta answered. "There's nothing but forest that way, and it will probably involve going up and down more hilly terrain. It's safer from a perspective of who we might run into, but not in terms of, well, wildlife."

Trudy nodded. No one had to specify exactly which form of wildlife they were afraid of meeting.

"So overall, that would probably be a shorter distance, but harder," Trudy said. "And potential dangers in either direction."

Axton rubbed his chin in thought as he mulled this over. In the end, he didn't have as much say in this as he probably thought he did, but it had kept him in line so far to let him think he was taking the lead. In truth, this was all Trudy and Gerta's show. Or really, just Gerta. Trudy would follow her recommendations long before she took anything Axton said seriously.

They were interrupted in their thoughts by a sharp whistle. Trudy looked up to see Isaiah at the edge of their clearing. He put a finger to his lips in a shushing gesture, then motioned for everyone to follow him. Gerta quickly repacked the map, and all of them, Bedford included, quietly came up to join him.

"What is it?" Trudy whispered.

"Fresh gorilla sign," he said. "Very recent."

Axton tensed. "No. We're not following any more gorillas. I already told you, this is all finished."

"I'm assuming you mean a normal-sized gorilla, correct?" Gerta asked him. "Not Gigantocus."

Isaiah nodded. "They are close. Less than half an hour walk, I would guess."

Trudy looked to Axton. "We can't ignore this."

"Oh yes we can."

"Irving believed in all this. He would have wanted us to still get as much information as we can before we leave."

"Unfortunately, Mr. Irving's opinion doesn't matter anymore," Axton said darkly.

"Wait," Gerta said. "Which direction were the gorillas heading, Isaiah?"

"North by northwest."

Gerta turned to Axton. "It would actually be on our way. All we need to do is follow them for a while, see if they're normal gorillas or these other, tool-making gorillas, and record anything we see if they are."

"It's only on our way if that's the path I decide on," Axton said. "And suddenly, I'm thinking the other way might be better. If these are, in fact, our special gorillas, then big old You-Know-Who can't be that far away. We're not going anywhere near them."

Trudy nodded to Isaiah. "Lead the way."

He started off with Trudy close behind. Axton grabbed her by the shoulder to stop her. "I said no. If you disobey me, you're not getting paid for any of this."

"Really, Axton?" Trudy asked. "You know better than anyone else that I'm not here for the pay. You saw my bookshelf. You saw my life's work. Being honest here, I've forced myself to live a hard life. There's really no telling how much more life this alcohol-drenched body of mine has in it. I could have decades, or I could die tomorrow of liver failure. So you'll pardon me if I do whatever I can to find a few more discoveries and make that life count."

"I'm going with her," Gerta said. "Which means you're choice is either to stay here and hope we come back, or come with us."

Axton grumbled. "If my employer wasn't already dead, I would definitely be saying that I was looking for a new job after this shit."

After five minutes, Isaiah showed them the sign he'd found in the form of broken branches and trampled grass. Something large had indeed come through here very recently. A few minutes later, they found a small amount of gorilla fur as well. When Isaiah looked at some of the signs and declared they'd come through here in only the last few minutes, Trudy took the lead from everyone else. In all truth, the gorillas in front of them probably weren't the ones they were looking for. Gorillas might not have been as numerous in the Virungas as they had been long ago, but their numbers had bounced back in the recent two decades thanks to conservation efforts and eco-tourism. It was more surprising that they hadn't come across any normal mountain gorillas yet at all, unless they somehow knew that this area now belonged to a group that was very, very different.

Trudy did her best to keep quiet as she moved forward, but she must have been out of practice. Something heard her and came charging out of the trees up ahead. She only looked at it long enough to know that it was a gorilla rather than something more likely to trample her like a Cape buffalo, then dropped her head and body low in a gesture of submission. She could hear most of the others do the same behind her, although she thought she only heard three other people join her in supplication. She was willing to bet that the one who refused was Bedford, but she didn't dare look up and back long enough to be sure. It was more important to let this gorilla know that she wasn't a threat.

For several frantic heartbeats, she didn't think the charging gorilla was going to stop. She had seen such a thing before, albeit rarely, and the results, while not usually deadly, almost always required emergency medical attention. The gorilla stopped, although not until she heard something else crashing through the brush nearby. Her curiosity overwhelming her, Trudy risked a look up.

The gorilla coming right for her had an axe in hand. The axe was raised over its head, clearly held up with the intent of it being a killing blow. This alone was startling and amazing, yet it still wasn't the thing that immediately grabbed all her attention. The only reason the gorilla had stopped charging was that another gorilla had appeared and rammed into it. The two gorillas looked at each other in a fierce moment of tension before the first one lowered its axe. The axe was a crude thing, made from chipped stone and a branch and tied together with dried vines, but there was no doubt that it had been put together with intention. The photos Irving had shown her were true. These gorillas had really and truly entered the Stone Age. They were no longer just using found objects as tools. They were making their own.

But it was the second gorilla that made Trudy's breath catch in her throat. He turned just long enough for Trudy to see his nose. She recognized that scar. There were other scars that had joined it over the many long years, but the main scar by which she had always identified him was still there.

"Kramer," Trudy said out loud, her voice in some bizarre place between a whisper and a shout. The gorilla turned all the way to look at her and snuffled curiously.

It was definitely him. He was much older, obviously, and the years showed. The coat at his saddle was now a complete and shiny silver. One of his arms didn't seem to move properly, likely the result a long ago fight injury that had never healed properly. Hell, for all Trudy knew, that could have been a battle wound from when he escaped the poachers. It would be a mistake to assume that she could read a gorilla's face in the same manner she would a human face, but she wanted to say that there was something hardened about him. Like he had seen some terrible shit and come out the other side with a bleaker view of the world. But that was ridiculous. She couldn't assume he might think that way.

Could she?

Kramer snuffled at her, took a couple of loping steps in her direction, and then seemed to think better of it. He turned back to the gorilla with the axe, made a couple of soft, hooting vocalizations, and then went in the direction the first gorilla had come from. The axe-wielder turned and followed him without any look back, as if they had completely forgotten that there were intruders in their territory.

The thick grass and brush and vines rustled as the two gorillas disappeared through it. Trudy didn't move. Her mind was racing so fast that she couldn't even identify any of the thoughts.

"Ho. Lee. Shit," someone said from behind Trudy. It took her a moment to recognize that voice as Axton.

"Oh my God. That was amazing!" Gerta said. "I've never, *ever* seen anything like that!"

"We can still follow them," Isaiah said. "If we keep our

distance, it looks like they will let us be."

"Are you crazy?" Axton asked. "Did you not see the part where the gorilla came at us with a fucking axe? We need to get out of here. Now."

"An axe that it appeared to make itself," Gerta said. "We need proof that it's true. If it is, then this changes everything we thought we knew about primates. The world needs to see and know this!"

"While I disagree with the reasons," Bedford said, "I do agree that we should follow. There is obviously something here that God wants us to witness."

"Trudy, please talk some sense into them," Axton said. "You haven't said anything yet. I know you're smart enough to be the voice of reason here."

Trudy didn't look back at anything. She simply stood up from her place on her knees and followed the two gorillas into the brush.

"Or not," Axton muttered from behind her. "You're fired. Gerta's fired. Isaiah's fired. Bedford would be fired if Irving's organization were actually paying him. Every single one of you is terrible at this."

Trudy trod carefully through the bushes and wild weeds, keeping a distance from the gorillas but always making sure that they were within her sight. She'd found Kramer for the first time in well over twenty years. He had answers to all the questions they'd been asking. She had no choice but to go. It was a compulsion. She couldn't have stopped her legs from moving even if she wanted to. And she certainly didn't want to.

She kept waiting for Kramer to look back, or even do anything at all to acknowledge that he remembered her. Gorillas certainly had good memories, but would he be able to recognize her, or did a gorilla have as much trouble recognizing a specific human after this long as a human would a gorilla? The other gorilla, still holding the axe, looked back several times and made motions like it wanted to go back and rip Trudy apart. Based on its coloring, this gorilla had to be either a mature female or a younger male. Probably a male, given its aggressiveness, but Trudy didn't want to assume. Every time Axe-Crazy (Trudy already found herself giving the gorilla a name, as inappropriate as it might be) tried to go back, though, Kramer cuffed the gorilla lightly and directed him to keep going. The path they went through went up a couple of steep inclines, and Trudy huffed and puffed as she tried to keep up. The others didn't dare get ahead of her, occasionally commenting on her eerie resolve, and soon were trailing behind her up the slope by about twenty or thirty feet. Trudy didn't dare slow down to let them catch up. She could not lose sight of Kramer.

The trees in this area thinned out to practically nothing, and the air was thin with the altitude. Trudy couldn't imagine where they might possibly be going, or even why it was just the two gorillas alone. When they disappeared over a hilltop and went down the other side, Trudy stopped for a few seconds to catch her breath. She really needed exercise. She also really needed a drink.

But even more than either, she needed to *know*.

Gerta caught up with her first. "Trudy, you have to slow down. You're going to give yourself a heart attack."

"This is hardly the most strenuous I've been since I got back to Uganda," Trudy said through a series of huffs. "You know that better than everyone."

"Are you okay?"

"Yeah. I've almost got my second wind, and then we can see if there's anything interesting over that ridge."

"No, I mean *are you okay*? Really?"

Trudy wasn't sure if Gerta was more concerned with Trudy's late-night confession or with her reaction to Kramer's sudden reappearance, although Trudy supposed they were linked close enough in her mind that it wasn't really possible to pull the two things apart.

"It's like I can have a moment of redemption here," Trudy said. "Do you understand?"

"I think I do."

"I need this. I'm used to doing these kinds of things alone. Except I don't think I want to do this one alone at all."

"I'll be right here," Gerta said, taking Trudy's hand. "Of course, it will pretty disappointing if we get over the hill and discover nothing more than more forest."

"That just means we'll have to keep following Kramer for longer," Trudy said. "Are you ready?"

"Absolutely."

Trudy looked back to see that the three men had stopped a short distance back. With Trudy's nod, they all started walking again until they reached the top and could look down over the other side.

"Well," Gerta said after several seconds of silent staring. "I can't really say I was expecting that."

Trudy had been doing her best not to expect anything at all. Even still, once she understood exactly what she was looking at, she had to say that it wasn't anywhere close to what she thought might be here, either.

The ridge they were on was particularly high, giving them a great view of the long-dead volcano beyond. The caldera could clearly be seen, despite being covered in forest and worn down to little more than a circular ridge surrounding one central spot. That alone wasn't anything particularly interesting, given the old volcanic nature of this region. The surprising thing was that, from this angle, they could clearly see that the whole interior of the caldera was hidden beneath a massive mesh of camouflage netting. From the air and satellite photos, Trudy had no doubt that it would look like more like open jungle. From this angle, below the netting, they could see poles holding it all up as well as what might have been a number of buildings.

"Did we just find a lost city or something?" Axton asked.

"Not in the classic Indiana Jones sense, no," Trudy said. "It looks to me like, whatever was built under there, it was put there recently."

"It still looks abandoned, though," Gerta said. "Look over there. You see how there's rips in the netting? Whoever put this here isn't here anymore."

Trudy glanced down the ridge to where the trees became more numerous again. She just barely caught sight of Kramer and Axe-Crazy disappearing back into the forest. She wanted to run after them, but she no longer thought that was necessary. If they kept going straight, then they would be heading right for the caldera.

"Whatever it is, that's where we're going to find our answers," Trudy said.

"Then does that mean we will also find Gigantocus in there?"

"Maybe," Trudy said. "Even probably. At the very least, it could tell us where he came from."

"Then here's an idea," Axton said. "How about we not go that direction?"

"It's man-made, Axton," Gerta said. "We might find something in there that we can use, like communications equipment."

"You people aren't even trying to be smart anymore, are you?" Axton asked.

"I have to know," Trudy said.

"I must say that I won't be satisfied until I know now, either," Gerta said.

"God has a plan for us here, Axton," Bedford said.

Everyone turned to look at Isaiah for his opinion. He simply shrugged. "Do not look at me. You foreigners are crazy. As long as I get paid when I get back and can tell my family what happened to my brother, then I will come along."

"When the hell did any of this become a democracy?" Axton called after them as they all started down the slope. After much cursing on his part, he had no choice but to follow again.

CHAPTER TWELVE
THE TEMPLE OF THE SACRED PAPER CLIP

Isaiah easily picked up Kramer's trail once again when they reached the trees, and from there, they continued on a more or less straight path to the caldera. Trudy figured they were going to have to climb yet another slope before they got in, but long before they reached the point where the land started to curve up again, they found what looked like a small, metal bunker. It had been built to stand the test of time and the elements, yet it had clearly been some time since any human had been here to check on it. Various plants and growth had started to creep up the sides, and the thick front door was wide open. Trudy went in first to discover that it seemed to be some kind of equipment shed. On the walls, she saw various packs and survival gear, all of it relatively new but disused. Trudy rummaged through some of the stuff, less concerned with finding anything that might be useful to them and more interested in looking for clues as to why it was all abandoned. In the back of the shed, there were stairs carved down into the volcanic rock, so while Trudy was busy with the supplies, Gerta found a flashlight and shone it down into the darkness.

"See anything?" Axton asked her.

"Yes. Rock. Lots of rock. But it's not what I see, it's what I thought I heard. I could have sworn I heard the echo of gorillas down there."

"That must be where Kramer and Axe-Crazy went," Trudy said.

"Axe-Crazy?" Bedford asked. "Is that really what you decided to name the other one?"

"It fit," Trudy said simply.

"It's probably a good thing you don't have children," Bedford said. "I can't imagine what you would name them."

Trudy stared at him. "Wait. Did you almost try to make a joke? Are you sure you're feeling okay."

"Ms. Hollis, I do believe I'm feeling better than I ever have before."

Trudy definitely did not like the edge in his voice. She let her attention go back to the supplies. "Everything looks mostly full. I can't really say whether a few things might be missing here or there, but there's a full pack at every hook. Whoever made this was prepared to get out of here in a hurry, and yet it looks like the left everything behind."

"Is there anything we can use?" Isaiah asked.

"Yeah, probably a few things." She pointed specifically at the machetes hanging on the wall. They were a little worn, but otherwise sharp.

"Wait, something about that doesn't sit right with me," Gerta said as she joined Trudy by the swords.

"What doesn't?"

"We've already seen that at least that one gorilla has a hand-made axe, yes? So why would it do that if there is a perfectly acceptable weapon right here?"

"They're hanging pretty high," Axton said. "Maybe they couldn't reach, or they just didn't see."

Trudy would have offered a comment on this, but her eyes fell on something else sitting on a high shelf. She froze and held her breath.

"Are you okay?" Gerta asked, seeing the expression on her face. Trudy simply nodded in the direction of the shelf. Gerta gripped Trudy's arm, telling her that the woman knew exactly why the sight bothered her. The rifle resting on the shelf under a thin layer of dust and dirt was the same make as the one that had been at the Cooper Memorial Zoo. Gerta reached up and grabbed it, also checking the shelf for ammo. There were tranquilizer darts up there, but not a proper weapon for them. After fumbling around for a bit, Gerta finally found a full box of bullets and set them down on a bench where everyone could see.

"Is there anyone here that knows how to use this?" Gerta asked. Trudy tried to hide her sharp intake of breath. Gerta knew damned well that at least one of them was very familiar with it.

Thankfully, Trudy didn't have to admit to anything. Isaiah picked up the rifle and inspected it, checking the attached scope to make sure it was clean and making sure that there was no bullet already in the chamber, then loading it.

"I can use this," Isaiah said. "Although it would be best if I took the time to clean it."

"I don't know that we should take that time," Gerta said. "If you had to use it on Gigantocus, do you think you could?"

There was a level of venom in Isaiah's voice that Trudy had not heard before. "Yes. Easily."

"Okay." Gerta took the tranquilizers and, after some thought, passed them out evenly among everyone so that they each had two darts. "These would probably be more effective coming from a gun, but since it looks like someone took it at some point, maybe everybody should have one or two."

Trudy inspected the darts in her hand. "Looks like exactly the dose that would be needed to take down a gorilla quickly without killing them. Whoever set this place up prepared specifically for that contingency."

"Does that give you any guesses what this place might be?" Axton asked.

"I'm starting to form a hypothesis," Trudy said. "But I could still be completely wrong. If you don't mind, I'm going to keep my theory to myself until I have more evidence."

Most of them stashed the darts where they could easily access them in pockets. Bedford was the only one who took longer to examine his.

"Is something wrong, Bedford?" Trudy asked.

"No," he said almost reverently. "Everything is exactly correct."

Trudy exchanged a look with Gerta. Obviously, Trudy wasn't the only one feeling especially uneasy with him.

"So now we have extra supplies," Axton said. "Enough for us to be safe on the whole trip back to civilization. Can we please go now?" He looked thoughtful for a second, then said, "Never mind. I already know that all of you are going to ignore my very sensible pleas."

"You've known us for so little time, and yet already you know us well," Gerta said. "Is everyone ready to continue?"

It was almost funny when a couple of them said they weren't, that they had to go to the bathroom first, but once they'd all gone back outside to take care of business, they once again congregated at the top of the stone stairs.

"Trudy? Do you still want to do the honors?" Gerta said.

"No, let me go first," Isaiah said. He had the rifle slung over one shoulder and his machete in the other hand. "I might be able to see something no one else can."

The rest of them each made sure they had their own machete, then they followed him down into the dark tunnel. It had been finished and strengthened by human hands, but from the winding and often organic path it took, Trudy guessed this had originally been a hollow lava tube that had just been repurposed. The floor was uneven in places, but they didn't have far to go before a thin light could be seen from the far end. There were some signs here and there of the gorilla's passage, but much of it looked like it had come from months ago rather than the last few minutes. Apparently, they had used this path quite often.

The tunnel ended in a door with one broken hinge. Inspecting it, Trudy figured this must have been some kind of emergency exit at some point. She was so busy trying to figure out what happened that, as she stepped out of the tunnel, she almost tripped on the bones.

"Ack!" she cried. The only thing that kept her from toppling over was Gerta's hand on her arm. Isaiah had missed the bones at first and needed to come back to inspect them. Gerta's feet had jumbled them up, but it soon became evident that they were part of a whole skeleton. A human skeleton.

"*Now* does anybody want to go back with me?" Axton asked.

Trudy bent down next to Isaiah, and they both examined the skeleton together. Although they were somewhat decayed, the skeleton's clothes still held it in some shape that still looked human. Most of the flesh had been eaten off by animals and insects by this time, but there were still a few mummified pieces clinging here and there to the bones. The skeleton wore jeans and a khaki shirt, and after poking around a little more, she also found it wearing a bra underneath.

"What happened to her?" Gerta asked.

"A better question is what happened to all of them," Bedford said as he gestured at the vicinity around them. They were in a nook at the bottom of a tall flight of stairs that led up to the top of the caldera. They were in the more-or-less open air now, with only the mesh on top protecting the area from the elements. From here, she could easily see a few areas where the mesh was ripped, leaving large gaping holes with the mesh gently flapping in the breeze.

All of these were the details Trudy noticed first, probably because her mind needed to take some time at first to process all the dead bodies.

Most of the ones she could see were strewn about on the stairs, the postures of the ragged skeletons giving the impression that nearly all of them had fallen over dead in the process of running down to escape. There were a few more on the ground level, now that Trudy forced herself to look. All were dressed similarly to the first skeleton and had roughly the same amount of decay.

"This is horrible," Gerta said in a low, reverent voice.

"God punished them for something," Bedford said. "This is his wrath upon them, probably for messing with forces that were none of their business."

"That's a lot of assumptions," Trudy said as she bent down to get another look at the skeleton. She took her pack off long enough to get a glove and a bandana. "Everyone, I would put something over your mouths," she said. "Just in case."

"Why?" Axton asked. Gerta and Isaiah, however, immediately did what she said and found some scraps of cloth or rags to put over their noses and mouths. Bedford and Axton reluctantly did the same a few seconds later.

Once Trudy had her bandana over her face and a rubber glove on her hand, she ran a finger in the dirt of the skeleton's clothes. Much of it was the grime and dust that accumulates with time, but just barely noticeable underneath it all there was a peculiar mustard-yellow dust.

"What is that?" Gerta asked.

"I don't know much about biochemical weapons, but my best

guess is that it's the residue of some kind of gas. I couldn't tell you which kind, if it were even something we'd recognize at all."

"Can it still hurt us?" Isaiah asked.

"I don't know. It might be inert in this form, for all I know. But I would be careful breathing around here, just in case."

"And let me guess," Axton said. "The presence of a possibly deadly dust all over everything *still* isn't enough to get us to turn back."

"You're catching on, Axton," Trudy said. She stood back up and forced herself to look at the bodies littering the stairs. "That would explain why it looks like they all died at once, and so quick. Somebody wanted them all gone before anyone could get out and tell the rest of the world about this place."

"But who did it to them?" Gerta asked.

"We probably won't have an answer to that question until we answer who *them* is in the first place," Trudy said. "I'm betting we're going to be seeing a lot more like this as we go. I hope everyone's ready."

The look in the eyes of everybody in the group told her that they weren't ready in the slightest, but they had to get moving anyway. Outside the alcove, they found a much more open area that let out onto what was more or less a small city. The buildings were all of some pre-fab design that had undoubtedly allowed them to be built quickly and with little fuss, although they were still sturdy enough that the multi-story structures would probably continue to stand for years to come. The mini-city was laid out in a basic grid pattern, with small structures near the outside and the taller ones toward the center, with the tallest being about eight or nine stories tall.

That one, out of all of them, seemed to have the most damage. Trudy pointed it out to Gerta. "Tell me something. What do the holes in the side of that building look like to you?"

Gerta answered immediately. "Hand holds. The hand hold of something very, very large."

Trudy nodded. There were thinking the same thing.

There were more skeletons in the street, although not nearly as many as had been congregating near the exit. This told Trudy that the people had probably had some kind of warning about what was about to happen, yet not enough for it to make a difference. The yellowish dust was more noticeable in places here, as well as clear paths through it that could only have been made by the repeated use of gorillas.

"If the gorillas aren't harmed by the dust, then it can't be harmful to us, right?" Gerta asked.

"Not exactly," Trudy said.

"But gorilla physiology is so close that human diseases can easily pass to them. Wouldn't it be the same with poison?"

"In most cases, I would think so. Unless this particular poison was specifically used because it would kill the humans but leave gorillas unaffected."

"But that's crazy!" Axton said. "Why would anyone want to do that?"

"Again, I've got theories," Trudy said.

"There is one simple way to settle part of this problem," Bedford said. Trudy turned just in time to see him pull aside the cloth on his face, stoop down to run his finger through some of the yellow dust...

...and then stick the finger in his mouth.

"You maniac!" Trudy yelled at him. "What the hell?!"

The deed was already done, though, and there was nothing for them to do but wait to see if Bedford started convulsing or barfing. After nearly a minute, Trudy let out a breath she'd been holding.

"You could have killed yourself, you idiot," Trudy said to him.

"God told me I was going to be safe."

"Yeah? Well, don't forget that I'm a Christian, too, and God told *me* that you're a dumbass." She ran a hand through her tangled hair. "Okay, so I guess that probably does answer that question. In dried powder form, whatever this stuff is, it must be inert. We're probably safe from it. But it might just be slower acting on the human body in this form, so just in case, everyone keep your masks on. And for the love of all that's holy, *please* no one else go *licking the fucking poisonous powder.*"

They wandered the streets a little more in silence before Gerta asked, "Okay, so what exactly should we be looking for?"

"Obviously any sign of where the gorillas might currently be, so we can try to observe them. Otherwise, one of these places around here has to be some kind of administration building. If there are any records as to what this place is and what they were doing here, that's where they would be."

"And if we suddenly hear the roar of a giant gorilla and the sound of it coming for us?"

"Simple," Trudy said. "Hide. And maybe pray, if that's your thing. Seriously, though, no splitting up."

They checked a few of the lower buildings, and while they didn't find what they were looking for, they still found plenty to fascinate them. A couple of the buildings appeared to be cafes, although all food in them had long ago perished or been taken. One, much to everyone's shock, seemed to be a movie theater. Trudy couldn't help herself but to check the upstairs projector to see what might have been playing, and found that the citizens of this place had apparently been in the middle of a Peter Jackson film festival. The closer they got to the center of the town, the more the buildings started to look residential. Some were little more than bunkhouses, but several were complete homes including amenities that would have been too rich even for Trudy at the height of her fame. After this, though, the buildings got taller and showed less personality. This, Trudy thought, was the best place to start looking.

"It's like a real town," Gerta said.

"This is more fancy than any village I have been to around here," Isaiah said. "I do not understand how this could have been here this whole time with no one seeing."

"Maybe it's placement at the border made it less likely that anyone would venture here," Trudy said. "Or, given how much money was obviously put in to creating this place, I wouldn't be surprised if the palms of certain government officials were greased to look anywhere but here."

Many of the buildings they passed now looked like they were warehouses. Most of them were still completely full of unopened crates, although Trudy took special notice of one or two that had been forced open and cleaned out of whatever their contents had been. Trudy took a closer look as some specks in the bottom of one of the crates, then abruptly stood up. "Crowbar."

"Huh?" Gerta asked.

"I need a crowbar. Or something to see inside one of these other crates. I think we've got it. I think this is the real answer we've been looking for."

"Great. Can we go now?" Axton asked.

"Shh," Gerta said. She looked around nearby, but there didn't seem to be anything for them to work with. Isaiah finally walked away long enough to find a rusting claw hammer, which he then handed to Trudy. She went to the nearest crate, took a moment to look around at the others expectantly, and then began to pry open the top. Gerta offered to help once it was partially pried up, followed by the rest of them each taking a part of the lid and hauling it up.

They dropped the lid to the side and all stared in.

"Son of a bitch," Trudy whispered reverently.

"I don't get it," Axton said. "It just looks like... what is that, sand?"

"No," Gerta said. "It's seeds."

Isaiah took a handful, sniffed it, and then tasted it. "Grains. I do not know what kind."

"Oh my God," Trudy said. "Oh my God, this is huge."

"Damn it, Hollis, don't try to tell me you don't keep doing this on purpose," Axton said. "You think you have some amazing discovery, but you don't tell any of us, like you think we should already know. Well, not all of us have an IQ of two thousand and fifteen, or whatever the hell it is you have. Just straight up tell us what this means."

"Huh. No," Trudy said.

Axton rubbed his head like he was developing a headache. "Of course she says no. Why did I think she would say anything different?"

"This still isn't the die-hard proof," Trudy said. "But I bet we'll be able to see that proof pretty clearly if we get a high enough view of the town. Come on. We're heading to that building in the center of the city."

The closer they got to the main building, the more Trudy felt a pressure growing behind her eyes, like this moment was too much for her tiny brain and it would burst at any time. She had a very good idea what she was about to see, but it was impossible. There was no way. Not in the stupidest, pulpiest science fiction would anyone have depicted something like this. Because it just wasn't something that was supposed to happen. There were some things humans did, and they were the only creature on the planet to do it. That was what was supposed to set humans apart from animals. Trudy, however, knew full well that gorillas could sometimes be more stereotypically human, while humans could be vicious, destructive monsters.

Everyone else seemed to feel the weight of this moment, as well. They all grew quiet except for Axton, who actually ceased his complaining for a few moments to let himself experience the awe of the moment.

"This is like one of those old adventure stories," Axton said. "The group of adventurers stumbling upon an ancient city deep in the jungle."

Trudy snorted. "Yeah, but in those stories, the adventurers are always a bunch of white people fighting against the evil hoards of dark-skinned people. The people who typically read that stuff would have a fit if they saw this group."

"True enough, but still," Axton said. "It's like there's a temple in the center of it all, and the lost treasure will be found in the center."

"Sure," Trudy said. "The Temple of the Sacred Corporate Office Complex."

"The other thing about those stories," Gerta said, "is that the temple is always full of traps. So I will be fine if we skip that part, thank you."

From the outside, Gerta's possibility sure didn't look likely. While it may have been the tallest building in this secret city, it was still as drab and pre-fab as possible. The outer walls were made of some of kind of gray plastic or stone, with only a few windows present on each floor. The enormous hand-hold gouges were the most attractive thing about it.

"Do you think it will still be safe to go up that thing, considering the damage?" Gerta asked.

Trudy shrugged. "I'm not a structural engineer. If it was Gigantocus that did that, it looks like he did the bare minimum he could in order to be able to climb it easily." She turned to look at Axton. Everyone else followed her lead.

"Uh, what?" Axton asked.

"I'm just waiting for you to object to climbing the tall building that could collapse at any time," Trudy said.

"And if I did do that, what would you do in response?" Axton asked.

"Probably something like this," Trudy said. She started walking toward what looked like the main entrance.

The inside of the building was quite dark, and they had to pull out flashlights in order to find their way around. This did indeed look like some kind of office building, complete with a lobby, a receptionist desk, and a waiting area. The interior stank with what Trudy knew to be gorilla shit. Given their typical habits, she had to guess that this was where any gorillas in the city typically slept.

Gerta sniffed. When Trudy shown her flashlight in the woman's face, Gerta was grinning rather than making a face at the smell. "That's more than a single nights worth of droppings," Gerta said. Anyone other than Trudy would have thought that was an insane thing to be giddy about, yet both of them understood what this meant. Gorillas didn't stay in one place, after all. They had to move to keep up with their scarce food.

Lots of gorilla shit meant food was not scarce. Whether or not Gerta had understood why Trudy was excited about the seeds earlier, she certainly was now.

They found a stairwell, and as they went up the various floors, the stink subsided. It wasn't that gorillas couldn't do stairs, but their short hind legs would make it difficult for them to climb up too far, and if there wasn't anything on the upper floors worth the trouble, the gorillas wouldn't bother. The floors were full of offices, boardrooms, record storage rooms, cubicles, and every other thing a typical office building could possibly need. What it didn't seem to have so far, though, were answers. Trudy stopped briefly in one of the records rooms, found an unlocked door, and leafed through one of the filing cabinets, but it seemed to be full of mundane things like purchase orders and employee paystubs. She was sure all of this could be a vital clue, but only if she had a massive amount of extra time to go through it all.

All of this was just the low-level stuff, anyway. She wanted to see any important files. She wanted to see the offices of the bigwigs. That was where she would confirm or deny her suspicions.

At the seventh floor, they all had to stop, as the door leading up to the last floor was locked. With the help of the claw hammer and a few carefully placed machete hacks, they finally managed to pry it open and get to the final floor.

The top floor was all just a single room, a large penthouse with windows on all sides. Most of the windows were shattered, and a stiff breeze blew through. They all stowed their flashlights again as they wandered around. Trudy had guessed right. Given the ritzy décor and furnishings, she guessed this was both the home and the workspace of whoever had been in charge here.

"What is it we are looking for here?" Isaiah asked. "I can track leopards for fifty miles at a time, but I do not think I will be much help looking for papers. It is not my expertise."

"Try to find a desk or something," Gerta said. "Maybe a work station. A computer perhaps, although without power I don't think we'll be able to get any information from it here."

"If we do find one, we could always take the hard drive and finally get out of here," Axton said.

"Trudy, what do you...?" Gerta stopped talking. She must have seen the way Trudy was staring straight at the wall of broken windows facing out away from where they had come. Trudy stepped slowly, unable to tell how she might react if she didn't see what she had believed to be there. Hell, she had no idea how she would react if she *did* see it.

"Trudy, wait." Gerta rushed up beside her and took her hand. "We'll go look together."

"Look at what?" Axton asked.

"A vision," Bedford said. He sounded just as enraptured as Trudy, although probably with very different motivations. "Over there we will see what God has meant us to see all along."

For once, Trudy didn't want to give him crap. Her belief in God might have been paper-thin, but if she was going to believe at all, she might as well believe that Bedford was right. This was what they were all here to truly see.

The group formed a loose line and walked up to the window, keeping just enough distance from the edge that no one would be injured by the broken glass or get caught in a stray wind to be thrown over the edge. They didn't need to get that close. The thing they had come here to see was large enough to take up most of their view.

It was a farm.

Not that it was a farm as most experienced human farmers would have recognized it. There was no barn, no farmhouse, no heavy equipment. The plants growing in it were not in straight rows or even always in any sort of logical placement at all. A small patch of something that looked from here like it might have been tomato plants were surrounded by a wall of corn, and wheat waved among cucumbers. Not all of the plants here had come from the crates, either. From this height, it was impossible to be sure, but Trudy thought she saw a large patch of wild celery, the seeds obviously harvested from the wild and brought here.

All of that was well enough, but the truly extraordinary part was the gorillas wandering among it all.

"No," Axton said. "They can't be doing what I think they're doing."

"They are," Trudy said. She could barely get the words out. Her breath caught in her throat, and she felt faint. "They're tending the crops."

"That's ridiculous," Axton said. "Animals can't do that."

Animals can't, Trudy thought, *but people could.* The mountain gorillas down among the small, haphazard field, could not, with any good conscious be considered mere animals anymore. Whether they had somehow discovered it by themselves, or someone had taught it to them, this group (she thought there might be six or seven of them, but she couldn't be sure this high up) now had one of the most important technological advances humans had ever achieved. Agriculture. They could control their own food source.

Trudy squeezed Gerta's hand, who silently squeezed right back.

CHAPTER THIRTEEN
GIGANTOCUS, LORD OF STONE

"I have spent my entire life finding gorillas for *muzungas*," Isaiah said. "I know there is more to them than some people think. But I never imagined this."

It was only when he said this that Trudy realized they had all been staring out the window in silence for several minutes. His words broke Trudy's reverie. "We still don't know how this happened," Trudy said. "There's got to be something around here that can tell us. Were they taught? Were experiments done on them? Everyone, look around. Find that information, and we can finally leave."

Gerta was the only one who didn't join the hunt for more information. Instead, she pulled out her camera and did her best to capture everything she could, despite details being scarce so high up. Isaiah and Axton looked in the area that might have been the bedroom, Bedford went to some place that looked like an office, and Trudy went to a series of high bookshelves that must have served as the library. Bedford came back to her several minutes later and reported that he had found nothing, although Trudy immediately made a mental note to look again when he wouldn't see. She didn't trust him. He'd been acting slightly more stable during the last few minutes, but it still seemed possible that he might discover something then try to hide it from her.

On a desk stacked high with books fluttering open in the breeze, Trudy finally found a file folder. She wouldn't have thought anything of it at first except for its peculiar color, a glossy, pale blue. When she pulled it out from underneath the books, a Post-It note came off and fluttered around on the floor for a moment before she caught it and read it.

Just in case, it said in hurried, jittery letters.

Gerta finished her photos and came over to join Trudy. "Did you find something?"

"Don't know yet," Trudy said. Underneath where the sticky note had been, there was a logo. It didn't look like much, just the words *Paperclip Unlimited* under a simplified line drawing of the titular fastener.

"Have you ever heard of a company or group with that name?" Gerta asked.

"No, but a company isn't going to build a secret installation in the middle of the East African jungle and then go offering their stock publicly on Wall Street," Trudy said. "This probably isn't even their real name."

She opened up the folder and read out loud the opening line on the first page.

"'If you are reading this, then I am dead.'"

"That's a bit of a cliché way to open a letter in a secret document, wouldn't you say?" Axton asked as he joined them as well. Isaiah and Bedford were close behind.

"I don't know about that," Trudy said. "It does get straight to the point." She continued reading. "'I don't know who might end up reading this, although I think it would probably be someone from Paperclip here to clean up the mess. It's even more likely though that this file will just sit in the humid Equatorial atmosphere and rot. I'm probably typing to no one. And if you are from Paperclip, you're just going to destroy this like every other piece of evidence you find. But if someone is reading this, and you're not from Paperclip, I'm sure you're wondering just what you've stepped into. I'm guessing there's probably bodies. I sure hope not. I hope that, whatever backup contingency Paperclip has in place, most of the good, hard-working people escaped from it. But I don't think I will get out with them. I fully expect you to find my body right next to this folder.'"

Trudy stopped and looked around. "Did anyone see a body in here?"

Everyone shook their head. Trudy shrugged and kept going. "'If you are reading this, then you are probably standing in a secret corporate facility dedicated to genetic research. I'd be lying if I said I knew much more than that, although I do know there have been others in the past and suspect there are currently multiple others throughout the world.'"

"Jesus, should I go get my tinfoil hat?" Axton asked. "Next this person is going to tell us about the dark secret behind chemtrails or some other conspiracy nonsense."

Trudy cleared her throat and read the next line. "'And no, before you ask, I can't tell you anything further about chemtrails.'"

Axton shut his mouth.

"'No matter how crazy that sounds,'" Trudy continued, "'I ask you to take a look around yourself. Unless someone got this file out of the facility, I suspect you've already seen more than enough to support my story.'"

"I would have to agree with that," Gerta said.

"'I'm writing and printing this out because I have just been informed that this project is being shut down. Given the rumors that I have heard about past installations, I'm led to believe that Paperclip Unlimited will take what they feel are necessary steps to keep people from talking. One of the Grandchildren themselves called me personally just now. I have never spoken to either of the Grandchildren. No one has ever spoken to the Grandchildren. Because of that, my best guess is that I don't have long to type this.'"

Trudy stopped and looked at everyone else. "Grandchildren. I have no clue what that means, but it certainly comes across as sinister to me."

"Like the Godfather," Axton said. "We may have stumbled across the Michael Corleone of illegal corporate genetics research."

Trudy quickly scanned the rest of the letter. "There's no other mention of them. If there's any other answers to be had about the Grandchildren or Paperclip Unlimited, we're not going to find it here."

"What else does the letter say?" Gerta asked.

"It references a thumb drive that was supposed to be with the folder. Whoever wrote this, they tried to print out a hard copy of everything they had, but wasn't sure if they would manage in time. Anything that didn't get printed would be on the drive, but I don't see one anywhere around here. Do you?"

They quickly checked the immediate vicinity, but found nothing. "Doesn't such a thing need a computer?" Isaiah asked. "I do not think I've seen one around here."

"No, I don't think I have, either," Trudy said. "Which is suspicious. I'd almost think someone came along and took it at some point."

"Yet they missed the folder," Gerta said. "Sloppy, but those kinds of people probably don't even think about bothering with hard copies anymore."

"If someone came back and cleaned the place out," Axton asked, "then why wouldn't they destroy all the other evidence? Why not destroy the entire installation?"

Trudy looked through the papers in the rest of the folder. "Because they wanted to get rid of everyone that knew about what they were doing here, but not the research itself. And while a lot of this stuff is a bit too technical for me to read, it looks like their research was Gigantocus."

"What about the farming? The agriculture?" Gerta asked. "Are they the ones that taught the gorillas?"

"Um, I don't think so?" She flipped through a few more pages before she found something that had caught her eye. "It looks like their work here was all about Gigantocus alone. Not only creating a mutant hybrid of modern mountain gorillas mixed with other DNA—look right here, one of their samples *was* supposed to be *gigantopithecus blacki*, but there were others in the mix as well— but it also looks like they were experimenting with intelligence." She closed the folder and looked reverently back out the window. "They were teaching him skills that humans first learned long ago in an attempt to see what they could do with evolution. They taught him about making tools, about agriculture. Then they died. He was left alone."

"He sought out the closest things to himself that he could find, didn't he?" Gerta asked. "He got lonely. He gathered up other gorillas."

"Other loners, gorillas that maybe had a reason to be squeamish and hide deeper in the forest, just like Kramer," Trudy said with a nod. "He formed a brand new group out them, and then he passed on what he had learned."

Trudy felt a slight shudder. If she wasn't so keyed up by all these revelations, she might have ignored it. Instead, she held up a hand for everyone to be quiet as she waited to see if she would feel it again. A few seconds later, she felt it again, but stronger this time.

"It's Him," Bedford said. He'd sounded worrying before, but now he was even worse, looking almost like he believed the Lord above would rapture him right here and now. "He's finally come for us."

"Gerta, stow this in your pack," Trudy said, holding out the folder. Gerta took it as Trudy approached the window again. "Everyone, stay quiet," she said.

The entire complex shook again. On the farthest side of the caldera, at a place where the mesh was ripped greater than in other places, a shadow blocked out the light from above. Gigantocus leaped down from the rim, catching an outcropping in the rock to slow his fall and swinging against the rock wall until he came to a rest on the ground. Trudy stared at him as he snuffled and looked around, but movement elsewhere caught her eye. "Isaiah, hand me the rifle," she said as quietly as possible. She hardly believed that Gigantocus would be able to hear them all the way here from that distance, but given that he was already the product of tinkered-with DNA, she had no idea what surprising capabilities he might still exhibit.

"Trudy," Gerta said. "Don't. Trying to shoot it would..."

"The scope," Trudy clarified. "I need the scope. There's something going on down in the field."

Isaiah held out the rifle, which Trudy took gingerly before carefully unclipping the scope, shouldering the rest of the rifle, and using the scope as a telescope.

"It looks like the gorillas are all on the move," Gerta said. "They're heading toward Gigantocus, but... why are they moving in such a staggered fashion?"

Trudy took in a sharp breath.

"What?" Gerta asked. "What do you see?"

"I think... I don't know. It looks like they might be, uh, supplicating themselves to Gigantocus? Bowing to him?"

"Praying," Bedford said. "They're praying to him."

Trudy took the scope away from her eye. "Yeah. I think maybe they are." Each of the gorillas had stopped what they were doing in the fields and started in Gigantocus's direction, but along the way they would stop every so often, lower their bodies ahead of them like they were stretching out, and then slapping the ground. It looked very similar to religious practices Trudy had seen in faiths around the world.

Gigantocus had gathered them all together in this special place where they would be safe from the outside. He had taught them how to build things. He had taught them to plant and grow. He had given them knowledge that significantly changed everything about themselves. And the gorillas, so like humans in so many other ways, had mimicked this one last practice that people like Bedford had assumed was beyond them.

They had created a religion. They believed Gigantocus was their god.

"I think it's time for us to leave," Trudy said softly.

"Finally!" Axton said.

Trudy turned away from the window. "We'll all head back down to the first floor. From there we'll..."

"*Hey! Over here!*"

They all turned and stared in horror at Bedford. The man had moved off to the side and stood at the edge of the broken glass, his hands cupped to his mouth to amplify his voice as he screamed out over the distance. There was enough space between them and Gigantocus that his voice could have easily gotten lost had the wind been up more, but Gigantocus suddenly turned his head in the direction of the central tower. They weren't going to be so lucky.

"Bedford, you idiot! What are you doing?" Trudy ran for him, but Isaiah was closer and faster. He made a move to grapple Bedford from behind. The preacher must have been expecting it, as he twisted and jabbed something into Isaiah's stomach. Trudy gasped as she thought for a moment that he'd stabbed Isaiah with one of the machetes. As Isaiah tried to pull away, though, Trudy saw that Bedford, while still holding the machete in one hand, had in fact attacked him with one of the tranquilizer darts. The tranquilizer did its work quickly, causing Isaiah to stumble toward the window. Axton got there fast enough to grab Isaiah and pull him back to relative safety.

Except relative was definitely the key word, as a forty-foot gorilla mutant was now charging towards the central building, its roars a clear challenge to the puny creatures that had dared violate its domain.

Trudy held back Gerta from going for Bedford as Axton dragged Isaiah's prone form back in the direction of the stairwell. Bedford still had one tranquilizer in one hand and his machete ready in the other. The last thing Trudy wanted to see was Gerta get her wonderful head chopped off.

"Bedford, what the fuck are you doing?" Trudy screamed at him. She had no choice but to yell. The din of Gigantocus rumbling toward them was making it hard to hear.

"This is it!" Bedford said. "This is what God wanted from me all along! Humanity has sinned once too often! The new flood has come to wipe away the perversion of people like you, except he has sent it in the form of man's own hubris."

"You moron! That's not even slightly what the hell is happening here!" Gerta said.

"Gerta, come on. We have to get out of here!" Trudy said, trying to pull her even farther away from the window. Gerta, however, looked like she'd finally had enough and was ready to shove him right out. Gigantocus disappeared from view as he reached the bottom of the tower, and the building's sudden wobble and shake told Trudy that he was already using his hand holds and coming up.

"He is returning to his guise from the Old Testament!" Bedford called, no longer so much to Trudy and Gerta as he was to anyone or anything that might be listening through the window. "No more will he send his son in a humble form to try to save us from ourselves. We had our chance, so now he comes in a new form! Humanity shall be wiped out and replaced by the next closest thing to us."

The building shuddered so that Trudy almost stumbled. Finally, Gerta seemed to realize that going after Bedford wasn't going to do any good, and the only choice they had left was to try to get somewhere Gigantocus wouldn't find them.

"Gigantocus is the Holy Spirit and God's wrath made flesh!" Bedford had turned now to look straight down the side of the building. What he saw put a look of hysterical glee on his face. "He will destroy us here, then he will go forth and destroy all the rest of the wicked. Everyone will go down to the fires of hell but those few of us who have seen his way all along!"

They were almost back at the stairs, but Trudy couldn't control herself as a shadow loomed up behind her, blocking the light through the window. She turned to look. Gigantocus loomed there, his face only partially visible through the narrow view of the window. The snarl he gave them was clearly angry, challenging, but it wasn't directed at Trudy and Gerta just yet. Instead, he looked directly at Bedford, who stood completely unafraid in front of the giant beast.

"Lord, you are my master and I give myself completely over to your infinite wisdom," Bedford said, partially to Gigantocus and partially to the open air beyond. "I accept your judgment on my poor, weak human soul."

Gigantocus snuffled. He actually looked for a moment like he completely understood what Bedford had said, and he wasn't entirely sure what to do. Hell, given what the letter had said, maybe Gigantocus *had* understood.

He snuffled again, then casually reached up to the window and gently took Bedford between his fingers. Bedford's face lit up with rapture as Gigantocus slowly pulled him out the window, being careful not to catch Bedford on any of the broken glass.

Then, without another glance, he let go. Bedford didn't scream, nor did he struggle. In those last seconds that Trudy saw him, he looked legitimately happy.

Gigantocus turned to look at Gerta and Trudy. Trudy started to run again, but Gigantocus moved too fast. With decidedly less care this time, his enormous hand shot through the window, his fingers whistling by Trudy's ear as they barely missed her.

They didn't miss Gerta.

As one finger wrapped around Gerta, Trudy slid to a halt just a few feet from the stairs. If she kept running, she was sure she would be safe. Axton had already taken Isaiah down, and she could hear Axton on the landing below, calling up to her and asking if everyone was okay. Trudy turned, trying to grab Gerta's hand, but Gigantocus pulled her just out of Trudy's reach. Much like he had with Bedford, he moved deliberately, as though it was very important to him that he not hurt these particular intruders by crushing them or bashing them against the floor and ceiling, but rather that they had to be picked out of his building like fleas on a dog and then chucked aside as meaningless, inconsequential vermin.

That was exactly it, Trudy realized. This place was his, and he didn't want to get any of their blood or guts on it.

Gerta screamed, still reaching for Trudy. Trudy's first impulse was to run for her, but a more logical part of her brain knew that such an effort would do nothing, that they wouldn't be able to pry Gigantocus's fingers from around her fragile form before he could get her to the window. Instead, she dropped down to one knee, unslung the rifle from her shoulder, and brought it up as she clicked the sniper scope back in place.

She only had seconds to do this. Any wasted moment would result in Gerta taking the quick way back down to the bottom. She lined up the rifle at the mutant gorilla's eye and looked through the scope, her finger ready and in place on the trigger.

And she stopped. Through the scope, all she could see was Killroy.

Of course, she knew it wasn't him. He was now stuffed and on display in some museum, an ignominious end for such a majestic creature. Gigantocus also had some clearly different structure to his face, evidence of all the genetic tampering that had been done to create him. But his eyes. There was clearly intelligence behind them. He would probably have been just as capable, or maybe even more so, of compassion in the sight of Trudy's misery like Killroy had been. Gigantocus was majestic, beautiful, a force to be reckoned with. He didn't deserve to be shot down here.

Or at least that was how she thought she was supposed to feel here. Instead, all she knew was that this gorilla didn't have some nameless child in his hand. He had Gerta. Trudy might not be able to say she truly loved the woman, but she cared. For the first time in many, many years, Trudy cared about a human more than she could care about a gorilla.

She fired.

The first shot hit him directly in the eye. He yowled, a horrific noise that echoed all throughout the caldera, and released Gerta. His hand was still so deep within the building that, in trying to extricate it, he got it caught on pillars and bookcases and furnishing. Even though both his eyes were now closed in pain, Trudy still had a shot on the other one. She supposed she didn't have to. Gerta was free. They could run. They could all hide for now, and then find their way out of the complex, down the tunnel to safety, and then back to some village or town while the enormous gorilla stayed behind, nursing his wound.

But fuck him. He'd gone after Gerta.

She fired again, shooting right through his other eyelid and blinding him in both eyes. The scream he made was indescribable, a sound of pure agony the likes of which Trudy had never thought she would hear. Although she couldn't see what he was hanging onto with his other hand, she knew he had let go as his head tilted back and his hand was ripped from where it had been caught.

Gigantocus fell from view. Even though she couldn't see it, everyone clearly felt the moment his body made impact with the complex below.

CHAPTER FOURTEEN
THE QUIET MOMENT OF NOW WHAT

Isaiah was in bad shape. The tranquilizers had been loaded with the proper amount to take down a gorilla instantly, so the amount that had probably gone into his system was likely dangerous to humans. Despite his fitness, his breathing was shallow, and they all knew that they didn't have to option of staying for long at all. Gerta now had enough information to pinpoint a more accurate placement of their location on the map, so she plotted out their next movements while Axton and Trudy rushed around finding materials to make Isaiah a makeshift litter. Once they had it put together, they strapped him down on it and carried it back down to the ground floor as quickly as they could, then made their way back to the tunnel. From there, the ground was smooth enough that it only needed to be pulled by one person at a time. Axton took it first and led the way, quite obviously anxious in his speed to finally get away from this place as fast as possible. Trudy and Gerta hung back just enough that they could have some privacy as they talked.

"I wish we didn't have to leave so quickly," Trudy said quietly. "There's still so much here. The gorillas should be observed. Gigantocus's body should be studied. There's probably much more that can be learned about this whole operation, from specifics on the experiment to who this company is and how they managed to pull this off."

"We can come back," Gerta said. "We know where it is now. We can find it again."

"Yes, we can," Trudy said. "And so can others. Maybe we shouldn't tell anyone about everything we found."

"Are you being serious?" Gerta asked. "People should see this. The world should know what is possible."

"But that's just it. The whole world will know. Not just the scientists and the eco-warriors, or anyone that would want to protect this place. There will be people like Bedford. They'll turn these gorillas into an agenda, or a tourist attraction."

"Trudy, are you forgetting that you are one of the pioneers of the concept of using eco-tourism as a force to protect the mountain gorillas?"

"No, I'm not forgetting at all. But I'm also remembering what happened to Group Kappa. I'm remembering that a couple people with a vendetta against me had no problem slaughtering a whole family. If we tell everyone what we have here and where to find it, we'll be putting a target on this place."

Gerta stayed silent in worried thought for most of the trip back through the tunnel, going up to Axton only to help him bring the litter up the stairs. Once inside the shed they did one more quick look around for supplies, then Axton was off ahead of them again.

"I don't know if I would feel comfortable staying completely silent about this, though," Gerta said.

"I didn't say we had to be completely silent. What we need to do is hide the location. We have plenty of other proof. We have another witness in the form of Axton, and also Isaiah if we can help him. You have all the pictures you took. And probably most important of all, there's that folder in your pack. You're going to need to protect that. If these Grandchildren and Paperclip Unlimited people find out we have it, well, we've already seen what they were willing to do to keep this quiet."

Gerta nodded in the direction of Axton ahead. "Do you think we can still get help and funding through Irving's groups?"

"Maybe. That will probably be a huge mess to clean up all by itself. At the very least, his name will lend some credence to everything that happened. It can attract a few other respectable researchers to help study it all. But not right away. These gorillas have a right to live for a while in peace before..." Trudy stopped and suddenly turned back in the direction of the shed.

"What?" Gerta asked.

"I thought I heard something." Trudy kept looking for several seconds, then gestured for Gerta to keep moving. "Must not have been anything."

"So what about you, then?" Gerta asked. "What are you going to do now?"

"I... I don't know. I still don't have anything to go back to. Maybe I'll come back here, if I can find a way to do it secretly. Or..." Trudy trailed off. She had a vague thought of what she might do, but she wasn't sure how Gerta might react to it.

Gerta, however, already seemed to know her mind. "Trudy. I like you very much. I have a deep respect for you. But we cannot be together."

Trudy nodded, trying not to look rejected. "Yes, I figured that."

"I have my own life, and we both know that, despite everything we have together, you wouldn't be able to find a place in it. I want a life that I can settle down to when I am not in the field. That would drive you nuts. You would just end up drunk in my house in Austria and antagonizing my husband."

"Unless you left him."

"Which I'm not going to do. I do not and will not ever love him in a way a wife is supposed to typically love her husband. But he is my deepest friend, and he is my partner."

Trudy nodded again. Deep inside herself, Trudy had already known all that. Even if she might want differently, Gerta's place in the world would never be her place.

But what, then, could her place possibly be anymore? Trudy didn't belong in the world as it now was. She belonged in huts beside Dian Fosse, in the fields of Rwanda trying to save people being hunted. She didn't belong in a world of Facebook and YouTube and memes that shamed her for things they couldn't possibly understand. Neither did she really belong in the cities of Uganda where, despite her fame, she was still considered an outlaw simply for being who she really was.

She had nowhere, Trudy realized. Nowhere at all, and no one.

Trudy heard the sound again from behind her. She'd fallen a few steps behind Gerta, so when she stopped to look, Gerta didn't immediately notice. She'd thought she knew before what the sound was, but without seeing, she hadn't any proof. She saw now, though. A gorilla had followed them this whole way, probably keeping just enough distance so that it wouldn't be seen while still not losing their scent. The gorilla came out of some particularly dense foliage and stared at Trudy.

Kramer.

They stood there in complete silence for several seconds. Then Kramer reached out his hand in her direction, one of his fingers extended like he was pointing.

Trudy remembered that gesture very well, and apparently, so did he. He really had remembered her all along.

She looked back at Gerta for a moment. It did not take long to make her decision.

Trudy held out her own hand, extending it to Kramer yet again in the pose reminiscent of the Sistine Chapel.

"Maybe there is a way you could come stay with me," Gerta said. "Maybe if we…"

She realized Trudy had fallen behind and turned to address her. Trudy was gone.

"Trudy?" Gerta asked softly.

There was no answer but a faint rustle of bushes and the gentle patter as a light rain once again began to fall on the Virungas.

"Trudy?" Gerta said again, louder this time. "If you stay out here, you won't have any booze!"

She didn't receive an answer.

"Gerta?" Axton asked from up ahead. "Is something wrong?"

"No," Gerta answered. "Nothing wrong." She went back to following him with a sad but knowing smile on her face. "Nothing wrong at all."